The Noblest Vengeance

Have Body, Will Guard Adventure Romance

by Neil S. Plakcy

Copyright 2013, 2020 Neil S. Plakcy. This book is a work of fiction. Names, characters, places, and incidents either are products of the author's imagination or are used fictitiously. Any resemblance to actual events or locales or persons, living or dead, is entirely coincidental.

All rights reserved, including the right of reproduction in whole or in part in any form. This book was originally published by Loose Id. Maryam Salim did an awesome job of editing this book, and the rest in the series. Kelly Nichols created the new cover.

Reviews for Neil Plakcy and the Have Body series:

"Never slows down" – Literary Nymphs Reviews on *Three Wrong Turns in the Desert*

"Plakcy's characters... charm" – Kirkus Reviews

"An engrossing writer" - Publisher's Weekly.

"Plakcy's Tunisia is the perfect exotic locale for your fantasy summer vacation, if you don't mind dodging an assassin or two along the way." – Dick Smart, reviewing for the Lambda Literary Review

This book is dedicated to Marc, of course. You are my guardian angel.

> *La mas noble vengansa es el perdon (The noblest vengeance is forgiveness)*
> *—Ladino proverb*

1 — Workout

Aidan Greene was so engrossed in the pictures on the laptop screen that he didn't notice his partner come up behind him. "What are you looking at?" Liam asked, looking over his shoulder. Their small mixed-breed dog, Hayam, hopped up from her place beside Aidan's foot and snuffled hello to her other daddy.

"Pictures of my cousin's son's bar mitzvah." Aidan pointed at the screen. "That's my Aunt Sophia, my cousin Ellen, and her husband, Barry."

"Facebook," Liam said, noting the heading on the screen. "For people with too much time on their hands."

It was an argument they had been having for a while. Since they had moved to Nice, where they had regular, fast Internet service, Aidan had begun connecting with old friends and family online, mostly through Facebook. After over two years away from the United States, he was feeling a bit nostalgic for his old life.

"It's not a waste of time," Aidan protested. With his parents both dead, all he had left were a mix of aunts, uncles, and cousins. When he lived in Philadelphia for a dozen years after college, he saw family often. Reading their online profiles and seeing their pictures made him realize it had been a long time since he'd seen any of them in the flesh.

It made him sad to keep missing family events—an uncle's funeral, the birth and bris of a cousin's son, so many other rituals.

"All that social-media stuff is for losers," Liam said.

"So your sister Jeanne is a loser?" Aidan asked. "She's on Facebook. Did you know her dog died last week? And your other sister, Franny? She's been posting videos of your nephew's softball games on YouTube. Not to mention Joey Sheridan—he's got a Pinterest page with photos of his workouts."

"Why are you looking at my family and friends?" Liam demanded. "What they do is none of your business."

"Excuse me?" Aidan said. "Joey's not my friend too? You ever asked him that?" Joey was an old friend of Liam's, still a SEAL. He had visited them when they lived in Tunis and, contrary to Liam's expectations, been fine to discover that his old buddy was romantically involved with another man. "And your family has nothing to do with me?"

"My family doesn't even know you exist. And I'd like to keep it that way."

Aidan stood up from the computer and confronted him. "Why? Do I embarrass you? Am I too gay?"

Hayam scurried toward the bedroom, her toenails clicking on the tile floor. "You are when you act like a drama queen," Liam said. "My personal life is my own."

Aidan shook his head. "You really are clueless, you know that? I *am* your personal life. I cook your meals and do your laundry and suck your dick. It doesn't get more personal than that, pal." Aidan pushed his palm against his partner's chest. Liam was wearing a cotton T-shirt, and through the fabric Aidan could feel the warmth of his partner's skin.

Liam grabbed his wrist and turned it—enough to immobilize Aidan, not to hurt him. But Aidan knew that grip and how to rotate his arm so that his elbow bounced against Liam's six-pack, startling him enough to release it.

Then they were wrestling in the middle of the living room, knocking aside chairs and the coffee table, each of them struggling to master the other. Aidan knew he was doomed to lose; Liam was so much bigger than he was, more muscular, with years of SEAL training. But for the past two years he had been exercising and learning the moves Liam used.

Anger was always a good workout tool for them. The adrenaline coursing through Aidan's veins made him stronger and more agile. And he wasn't above playing dirty, either. He reached up under Liam's T-shirt, caught one of his partner's nipple rings in his fingers, and twisted.

Liam yelped and pressed his stiff dick against Aidan's thigh. Liam knew Aidan's weakness—he was a horndog, ready for sex after a single touch. And Liam was quite willing to exploit that. As Aidan wiggled to escape, Liam leaned down and kissed him hard, and Aidan gave up, melting into his touch.

With one meaty hand, Liam slapped Aidan's butt, hard. "That'll teach you," he growled when he broke the kiss. "Don't fuck around with me."

"Seems like that's exactly what we're doing," Aidan said, panting slightly. "Fucking around." He stroked Liam's dick through his silky gym shorts.

Liam released his grip on Aidan and stepped back. "No, just teaching you a lesson," he said. "Now come on, we've got to get ready. We have a client today, remember?"

"Liam," Aidan said, dragging the name out. "You're not going to leave me here like this, are you?" He pointed down to where his dick pressed against his shorts. He could feel a wet spot growing on his boxers.

"I'm going to take a shower," Liam said. He pulled his T-shirt up over his head, exposing his bulging chest and improbably narrow waist. Then he dropped his shorts to the floor, leaving him clad only in his white jockstrap. His dick, stiff as well, pushed the pouch forward. "You can stay here. Or you can join me."

He dropped the jockstrap and his dick pronged out. He stepped nimbly out of the waistband and raised it to twirl on one finger.

"I'm right behind you," Aidan said.

"Just where you belong," Liam said with a wicked grin and then hurried toward the bathroom.

Aidan shucked his clothes with record speed and hurried behind his partner, who had the shower door open and the water cascading. Liam stepped inside, and Aidan followed, crowding against his partner's warm, damp flesh. They stood together, faces turned up to the water's flow as it streamed down over them. Aidan used the bar of lavender-scented soap to lather his hands, then placed them on Liam's chest.

He looked up to see Liam smiling at him, and that smile was almost enough to push him over the edge. Instead he focused on washing every inch of Liam's suntanned flesh. He was Irish American, with dirty-blond hair and skin that might once have been fair, before long exposure to the sun.

Aidan tried to remember the name of each muscle he caressed as his partner stood at parade rest beneath the stream. Latissimus dorsi. Rectus femoris. External oblique. But he always lost track somewhere after gluteus maximus as he worked himself into a frenzy.

He stood and reached for the spray adapter to rinse Liam, but his partner stopped him and instead took the soap from him. Then it was Aidan's turn to be lathered up, to feel Liam's rough hands touch him in every private place. When Aidan was covered in suds, Liam put down the soap and wrapped his arms around his partner.

They began to sway together to a melody that only the two of them could hear. Liam's dick rubbed against Aidan's belly, Aidan's dick against Liam's thigh. They kissed as the water rained down on them. Aidan could barely breathe from the pressure of his orgasm building inside him, and he clenched his eyes shut and sped up his rhythm, desperate for release.

Liam must have felt the same way, because the two of them pressed and rubbed until the soapsuds were gone and they were skin against skin. Aidan's pulse raced and he saw stars behind his eyes, and then his ejaculation burst out, followed a moment later by Liam's.

They slumped together against the wall of the shower. "I still think Facebook is for losers," Liam whispered into Aidan's ear and then turned beneath the spray.

A half hour later, after cleaning up in the shower, drying off, and resting on their king-size bed, Hayam snuggled by their feet, Liam sat up. "We have a dossier on this client?" he asked.

"Yup. I haven't had a chance to look at it yet, though."

"Why don't you do that while I take Hayam out to pee?"

At the sound of her name, the little dog lifted her fuzzy face. She had a soft, fluffy coat the color of very light coffee, a square head with a patch of white around her black nose, and another white patch under her neck. She weighed about twenty pounds and still had the endless energy of a puppy.

Aidan stayed in bed an extra minute while Liam dressed. At six-four, with bulging muscles, Liam looked every inch a bodyguard. He put on a black polo shirt that clung to him like a second skin, and Aidan noticed the way his twin gold nipple rings pressed against the fabric. His black silk slacks were creased thanks to the ministrations of the dry cleaner around the corner, his black loafers polished to a shine. He wore a gold chain around his neck, which matched one of Aidan's, and a gold watch, bought long before when he was a Navy SEAL and only recently brought out of safekeeping.

"Come on, get your cute butt out of bed," Liam said as he scooped up the little dog in his arms. She wiggled happily, trying to sniff him.

Aidan got up and put on his own black polo and slacks, along with the gold chain that matched Liam's. He was three inches shorter and a lot less muscular, but he still felt good about his appearance. He didn't fill out his black polo or slacks the way Liam did, but privately he thought he'd fit in better in the exclusive shops in Cannes, where they were headed. He and Liam made a good pair that way; Liam was the obvious muscle, sending a message to any possible bad guys. Aidan was more of a stealth bodyguard, fitting into the client's retinue unobtrusively.

He went back to the laptop computer, where he closed out Facebook and opened the dossier that their boss at Agence de Securité had e-mailed. Isa bin Khalifa Al-Nayahan was a member of the ruling family of Abu Dhabi, who were estimated to have a collective fortune of one hundred fifty billion dollars. He was involved in the country's oil business and was in Nice to negotiate a contract with a French company that sold refining equipment. He had brought with him his wife, Khadija, and their five daughters, all of whom wore the abaya, a neck-to-toe black robe, and a *sheela*, or head scarf.

According to the dossier, Al-Nayahan was worried about the rising anti-Muslim sentiment in France, which had included harassment of women in traditional garb, and that was why he had requested bodyguards to accompany his wife and daughters on a shopping spree. Their names were Abidah, Bahiyah, Durriyah, Fadiyah, and Ghaniyah, and they ranged in age from fifteen to seven.

Their primary destination was Cannes, where they had a list of stores they wished to visit. A limousine would pick them all up at ten at the Hotel Negresco, where the family was staying, and return them to the hotel no later than five o'clock. They had stated a preference for female bodyguards, but none were available, and with the husband's permission, Aidan and Liam had been assigned to the job because of their familiarity with Arab culture, after their years in Tunisia. Though the family's native language was Arabic, they were all said to be fluent in English.

When Liam returned with Hayam, Aidan told him what he knew and then asked, "What do you call people from Abu Dhabi, anyway? Abu Dhabinese? Abu Dhabians? Ibbity-bobbity-boos?"

"How about citizens of the United Arab Emirates," Liam said drily.

"And wasn't Abu the name of the monkey in *Aladdin*?"

"Let's go, Aidan."

They left the dog snoozing in a patch of sunlight by the French doors and walked out to the lobby, where Madame Serroli, the Italian-French concierge, reigned behind a half-round desk. Out on the street, the buzz of French life was all around them, from the slim women in pencil skirts who spoke animatedly into cell phones, to the teenagers in fake logo T-shirts and imitation sneakers lurking at street corners. People still smoked in France, and the scent of unfiltered Gauloises wafted past along with automobile exhaust and the latest single from Joe Dassin.

"Will we be able to talk to them?" Aidan asked as they walked. He knew that in many cultures women were not allowed to be around men who were not related to them.

"The Emirates are one of the more open Arab societies," Liam said. "Their constitution guarantees equal rights to men and women. Women can go to college and get jobs. And yes, they can talk to us."

The Negresco was a huge white hotel in the Belle Epoque style, with a pink roof and a central tower. They stepped from bright sunlight into a cavernous lobby with a domed ceiling and marble floors. Huge oil paintings rested in niches along the walls, and vast white chandeliers hung over groupings of ornate chairs and tables. They crossed the marble floor to the concierge desk and asked the young woman there to let the Al-Nayahans know they had arrived.

"The *sheikha* will meet you here within a few moments," she said after making the call. "Please, enjoy our seating."

Aidan made a mental note that Mrs. Al-Nayahan was to be called sheikha, and strolled over to examine one of the paintings, a happy-looking woman on a swing in the style of Fragonard. Liam could not be distracted; he assumed a military stance and faced toward the elevators, waiting for the Al-Nayahans to appear.

Aidan had enjoyed settling into Liam's life in Tunis, and the small house behind the Bar Mamounia. Sometimes he felt that leaving Tunisia had been a mistake—they were so happy there. But when the offer had come in from the Agence de Securité, Liam had been eager to make the move. The Arab world could be a dangerous one, for foreigners, Jews, and gay men, and Aidan remembered often worrying about their future there.

Hence Liam's push for the move. Their boss's wife had found and furnished an apartment for them, and they had begun working as employees rather than freelance contractors. They were regularly sent updates on trouble spots in Europe and had spent many hours familiarizing themselves with the area around Nice—the hospitals, police stations, major highways, the elegant hotels and high-priced restaurants where their clients might stay and dine. They had rehearsed the drive from the airport into the city and spent time among the luxury yachts at the Port Lympia, on the edge of the old part of the city.

"Here they come," Liam said, and Aidan turned to see a substantial woman in head-to-toe black emerge from the elevator, followed by five smaller versions of herself—like ducklings trailing their mama.

Liam and Aidan approached and introduced themselves. "I am very pleased to meet you," Sheikha Al-Nayahan said in British-accented English. "I believe my husband has a car waiting for us." She nodded toward an older Frenchman in black livery.

The driver led them all outside, where an extended limousine was waiting. As he opened the rear door for the women, however, a Frenchwoman in her fifties passing by stopped to stare at them.

"*Espèce de salope!*" she said, and she spit toward the Al-Nayahans.

Aidan was surprised to hear such a nasty curse coming from someone who looked so innocent, and realized this assignment might not be as simple as he'd thought.

2 – Nagging Feeling

Liam stood guard beside the open door of the limo as Aidan hurried the sheikha and her daughters inside. He stared impassively at the Frenchwoman, who continued to hurl curses as a small crowd gathered behind her. Between strings of invective, she lamented the death of her son, a French soldier, to "dirty Arabs" in Africa.

The humid air felt charged with electricity, and though Liam sympathized with the woman over her loss, he worried the crowd could get ugly, and he was relieved when the family was safely inside, and he could slip into the limo beside Aidan.

The chauffeur closed the door. "So this is what worried my husband," Sheikha Al-Nayahan said. She and her daughters clustered on the other two seats. The older girls looked nervous, the younger ones watching everything.

"I'm very sorry," Liam said. "That shouldn't have happened."

"Do you believe there will be more trouble in Cannes?" she asked. "Perhaps we should adjust our plans."

"I believe that was an isolated incident," Liam said. "In the middle of her yelling, I caught a few words. It appears that her son was a soldier, and he was killed in Africa."

"But we are not from Africa," one of the girls said. Liam thought she was the middle one, Durriyah.

"They do not know anything about us," the oldest girl, Abidah, said. "They think all Muslims live in caves and kill for sport." She turned to Aidan and Liam. "Is it true, that girls here cannot wear the abaya?"

"The law refers to all religious wear," Aidan said. "Christian, Muslim, Sikh, and so on. And only in schools."

"I would love to go to school here," the second girl, Bahiyah, said. "If I could, I would never wear this silly thing again." She turned to her mother. "Can we buy any clothes we want, *Ommi*?"

"Anything that I approve," her mother said.

Once they were underway, the girls relaxed and chattered among themselves, moving easily between English and Arabic. Fluent in Arabic, Liam was able to follow almost everything they said, most of which was about which shops they planned to visit and what they wanted to buy. He suppressed a smile; they would have been embarrassed to know that he knew all the words for undergarments in Arabic.

The boutiques would be simple, from a security standpoint. Dior, Chanel, Louis Vuitton, and the rest all had their own security, and there was little chance that the Al-Nayahans would be bothered. But the girls were also eager to visit the Cannes outpost of Galeries Lafayette—the big Paris-based department store—and that would be more complicated.

He gathered, from conversation between Aidan and the sheikha, that inflation was very high in the United Arab Emirates, so that even though there were many high-end stores, it was better to shop abroad when they could. "Especially when our goods will be tax-free," she said. "I must remember to collect the forms after each purchase."

Liam thought it was funny that a family who could afford a stay at the Negresco, a stretch limo, and bodyguards would care about saving a few euros here and there.

The limo moved smoothly through traffic on the oceanfront road. At Saint-Laurent-du-Var they turned inland to the A-8 highway, called La Provençale. The foothills of the Alpes-Maritimes were on their right, wearing their summer coats of dark green interspersed with lavender. As they passed Cros-de-Cagnes, Liam recalled a Renoir painting of the hilltop town that Aidan loved. Ocher towers of the churches were barely visible in the midst of bushy olive trees, the purple slopes of the mountains in the background.

The highway turned back toward the ocean after Cagnes-sur-Mer, passing the expanse of the Hippodrome de la Côte d'Azur. Liam hoped someday they'd get a client who'd require bodyguard services there; he'd loved going to the track in the States and even the camel races in Tunisia.

They exited the highway at the Avenue du Campon and drove down through the suburban sprawl of Le Cannet on their way into the center of Cannes. As they turned onto the Croisette, the oceanfront promenade made famous by the film festival, the girls tumbled over one another in their eagerness to look out the windows, even the more serious Abidah.

In boutique after boutique, Sheikha Khadija supervised her brood in the purchase of dresses, blouses, skirts, and shorts that no one outside their immediate circle of friends would ever see. They bought sunglasses and jewelry, makeup and accessories. At each stop the limo's trunk got fuller and fuller, but they avoided any problems.

The Galeries Lafayette was a four-story white building on the rue du Maréchal Foch, with wrought-iron balconies and red hanging banners. Inside, it resembled any upscale American department store but with French signage. The girls chattered eagerly, and Liam and Aidan struggled to keep them all together.

The girl behind the makeup counter, who couldn't have been more than eighteen, gaped openly at the flock of black-suited women who approached. Liam was afraid she would say something unpleasant, but quickly an older woman with tight skin shooed her to another counter. That one, he thought, could see money when it approached her.

Aidan remained at the counter with the sheikha, while Liam followed the five girls to the prêt-à-porter department of young women's fashions. They tried to scatter, but Liam said, "Girls! Please, stay together!"

It was like herding cats. Ghaniyah, the baby, was the worst. Every time her eye caught something, she took off toward it, and Liam had to jump in front of her, moving her back to the flock without actually touching her. The two older girls wanted to look through lingerie, and he was relieved when Aidan and the sheikha joined him.

Durriyah, Fadiyah, and Ghaniyah had armloads of blouses, skirts, and dresses, and they wanted to go to the dressing room. He followed them to "le dressing," hovering behind as they approached the twenty-something fashionista who guarded the door.

"Non, mademoiselles," she said, shaking her index finger. She told them they could not enter the dressing rooms in their voluminous robes. They could be thieves!

Liam looked around for another salesclerk, one who might have a bit more understanding of cultural norms. Durriyah began arguing with the girl in French while her younger sisters chimed in with words of Arabic. A couple of other customers stopped their browsing to look.

Finally Liam spotted a salesclerk with iron-gray hair marcelled into tight waves and a pair of pince-nez hanging on a chain around her neck. "*Madame, s'il vous plaît*," he called.

She swept across the floor to them. "Perhaps I can aid you," she said to the girls in French. "Let me come to the room with you and help you change. I know these robes can be very cumbersome sometimes."

Liam looked around. The other shoppers had returned to their browsing, and the girl to organizing a rack of returned items. When the sheikha and the older girls joined them, the same clerk helped them all, and Liam hoped she got a commission on her sales for her trouble.

There were no more incidents, but Liam couldn't shake a nagging feeling that something might go wrong. He thought about the few times when his own family had gone shopping together—his mother, father, and two younger sisters. There was never enough money in the McCullough household, because his father had drunk away his salary, so shopping was always difficult.

Liam had learned early not to ask for anything. He waited until his mother had noticed he'd outgrown his pants, or that his shoes had worn through their soles. His sisters, though, never caught on, and in the grocery or the mall they'd be whining and asking for candy, toys, or clothes. The trip usually ended with his father blowing up, often at the cash register. He could remember many times when they'd simply walked away without buying anything, leaving what they'd picked up in a heap at the register.

He was relieved when the family finally returned to the Negresco. By then it was late evening, and Liam realized why he'd been so on edge all day. His mother. "You know where the laptop is?" he asked. "I need to make a Skype call."

Their assemblage of computer-related products continued to grow. Each had a smartphone that could take pictures and give directions, among a multitude of other functions. Aidan had a Windows-based laptop, with the Skype software already installed, and Liam a MacBook. There was also an iPad, a pair of iPod touches for running, and Aidan's Kindle for reading.

"It's on the counter in the kitchen. Who do you have to call?"

"My mother."

Aidan looked at him. "Your mother knows how to use Skype?"

"Jeannie must have taught her. Now she wants to do video calls. Of course, I have to call her first on the phone to tell her to turn the computer on, which defeats the purpose, if you ask me."

"But with Skype she gets to see her Sonny Boy's face," Aidan said.

"I never should have told you she calls me that," Liam grumbled as he opened the apartment door. It was cocktail hour back in New Jersey, which was a good time to catch his mother at home.

His father had started to drink as soon as he got home from his factory job, and on through dinner and then the rest of the night. His mother managed with one dry martini, two olives. Even after his father had slammed his car into the back of a semi on the Jersey Turnpike, drunk out of his mind, his mother had continued the custom.

Aidan was in the bedroom packing their clothes. Liam carried the laptop to the living room and initialized the software, at the same time calling his mother. "Mom? It's me. You want to try this Skype thing?"

"I've got the computer right here. Just stay with me until I'm sure I've got you."

More quickly than Liam expected, his mother's face blossomed on the screen in front of him. Doris McCullough had always been a beautiful woman; she had even done some modeling as a young woman. She was slim and small-busted, tall for a woman of her era at five-ten. Pictures of her from back then showed long, straight blonde hair parted at the center, a small nose, and bow-shaped lips.

Her hair was still blonde, and Liam had no idea if she dyed it. She kept it in a big bouffant, lacquered in place with enough hair spray to poke its own hole in the ozone layer. She wore shiny pink lipstick that never left a mark when she kissed her only son.

Liam took after his father—Big Bill had been tall and broad-shouldered, with the same dirty-blond hair. When he looked in the mirror, sometimes he thought he caught a glimpse of his father in the way his hairline had begun receding.

"Oh my," his mother said when his picture had been transmitted to her. "You look just like your father."

"Not a good way to start a conversation, Mom," he said.

"Oh please," she said. "Your father may have been an alcoholic and an asshole, but he was still a helluva good-looking man. You must have women falling all over themselves there in France. At least you got out of that third-world hellhole you were in."

"How've you been, Mom? You feeling all right?"

"My right hip is still giving me problems. The doctor wants me to get a replacement, but I don't want to get into all that." She peered forward, as if she could look directly through the screen at him. "You look good, Sonny Boy. You staying healthy?"

"Yeah, Mom. I take my vitamins every day."

"Remember those Flintstones ones I gave you kids?" she asked, sitting back. "You would never eat the ones shaped like Wilma or Betty. You said they were for the girls."

"My vitamins now don't come in shapes. How are the girls, anyway?"

"Jeannie's been kind of down lately. You heard about Buddy, right?"

It took Liam a moment to remember Buddy was his sister's German shepherd mix, and that Aidan had mentioned the dog had died. "Yeah. Shame about him."

"She needs to get married again. Wasting all her time with that damn dog."

Jeanne was twice divorced, so Liam thought remarriage probably wouldn't solve all her troubles. "She going to get a new puppy?"

"Already did. Picked one up at the pound yesterday. I told her she was making a damn mistake, but she never listened to me. None of you kids ever did."

"Yeah, Mom, heard that song and dance," Liam said. "How's Franny?"

"At least one of my kids figured out what sex was for," Doris said. "I got two beautiful grandchildren out of the deal."

Liam remembered what else Aidan had said. "Tommy's playing softball, right?"

"Star of the team," Doris said. "Just like you were."

Aidan passed behind him, carrying one of their suitcases. Doris must have seen him, because she asked, "Who's that with you?"

"One of the other guys. We just finished a job, down the road in Cannes. That's in France."

"I know where Cannes is," she said, pronouncing it *canz*. "I'm not some homebody in New Jersey. I went on a cruise with the altar society at Our Lady of Perpetual Sorrow."

"Yeah, you're a regular world traveler. Listen, Mom, I've got to get back to work. Lots of things to wrap up."

"Aren't there any women bodyguards that work with you?" she asked. "Seems like you might need them."

He and Aidan had worked with one, a hard-bitten middle-aged woman, a former flic with a bad attitude. "Yeah, Mom, there are women bodyguards. But this job was just the two of us. Say hi to the girls for me."

He closed the connection before his mother could say anything more.

"Women bodyguards?" Aidan asked from behind him. "Really? Your mom is still trying to fix you up with a girl?"

"I ignore her," Liam said.

"So you've never said anything about me to her?"

Liam turned to look at him. "What I do in my personal life is my own business."

"Do you think you'll ever come out to your family?"

"Why is that an issue? We live a thousand miles away from them."

"It's not an issue, Liam," Aidan said in that prissy tone he used when something really was a problem despite his denials. "I just don't think of you as a guy who's afraid of very much."

"I'm not afraid of my mother," Liam said.

"Of her disapproval, then," Aidan said.

"Please, spare me the amateur psychology."

Aidan snorted. "Does she still call you Billy?"

Liam had been born William James McCullough, only his middle name distinguishing him from his father. He'd always been called Billy or Little Bill as a kid. When he left the military, determined to make significant changes in his life, he'd switched to the name Liam. His mother and sisters and a couple of friends from the SEALs were the only people in his life who still called him Billy.

"Of course she does. I've never told her anyone calls me anything else."

Aidan shook his head and walked away. Liam thought about chasing after him, defending the choices he'd made with his life, but that was a fool's game. Aidan had been out to his parents since college, but they were an upper-middle-class family, both parents college educated, so they'd been willing to accept the idea of a gay son.

Liam yawned and realized it was late, and they'd both had a very active day, between running and working out and then preparing for departure. He stripped down, used the bathroom, then joined Aidan in bed, where his partner was sitting up reading something on his Kindle.

They'd just had sex that morning, but Liam had an unreasonable urge to prove he wasn't the wimp Aidan thought he was. He reached over and grabbed Aidan's limp dick in his fist, squeezing and waiting for it to get hard.

"Liam, I'm reading," Aidan said. "And we had sex this morning."

"What? You're not horny for me?"

"Not when you're trying to prove something."

Liam took his hand away. "I'm not trying to prove anything."

"Sure you are. You worry that I think you're a pussy because you can't come out to your family."

"Excuse me?" Liam said indignantly, crossing his arms over his chest, even though his partner had read him clearly.

Aidan turned off the Kindle and placed it on the bedside table, then turned to Liam. "You have the right to decide who you come out to and when. I've never pressured you about that."

"You sound like a damn therapist," Liam grumbled.

Aidan slid down in the bed and rested his head on Liam's chest. Liam reached around his partner and pulled him close. Aidan yawned, then said, "I love you, sweetheart."

"I love you too," Liam said. Within moments Aidan's breathing indicated he'd fallen asleep, but Liam stayed awake, watching the numbers change on the digital clock and thinking about families. He had the nagging feeling that the issue of coming out to his family—which had been on a low simmer for a long time—was going to come to a head the more Aidan interacted with his own family.

3 – Family Matters

Aidan woke to Liam standing beside the bed, wearing a tight tank top and equally tight nylon shorts. If it weren't for the jockstrap beneath the shorts, the view would have been indecent. "I'm going for a run," Liam said. "Want to come?"

Aidan sat up and stretched. "Sure. Can you take Hayam out to pee while I get ready?"

Liam put his hands together and faked a bow. "I am your humble servant." He clicked his fingers together, and Hayam jumped up from the floor and began to dance around him.

"You may be a servant, but you're anything but humble," Aidan called as Liam walked out, the dog at his heels.

Aidan put on a jockstrap, his running shorts, a T-shirt, socks, and sneakers and was already stretching when Liam returned. After a little more than a year in Nice, they had a regular run: down to the oceanfront, along the Promenade des Anglais, then turning onto the Quai Lunel, which ran beside the port. When they reached the church of Notre-Dame-du-Port, they turned around and retraced their steps, continuing as far toward the airport as they felt like, then circling back home.

It was a hot morning in mid-July, and only the ocean breeze made the run bearable, even at eight in the morning. They ran past the entrance to Vieux Nice and the open-air market at the Cours Saleya, brilliant with fruit and flowers. An old schooner with tall masts was docked at the port beside some billionaire's gleaming yacht. All the contradictions of Nice, old and new, in one run.

At first, Aidan had only run as far as the market with Liam, waiting for him to circle back. But gradually he had worked up his endurance level to where he could match his partner.

They were home again by ten, to the ringing of the phone. It was Jean-Luc Derain, their boss at the Agence de Securité. "Sheikha Al-Nayahan was very pleased with the way you handled yourselves yesterday."

"We aim to please," Aidan said. "Any new work for us?"

"Nothing at present," Jean-Luc said. "But I will let you know if anything comes up."

Aidan thanked him and hung up. One of the nice things about working for the Agence was the ability to relax when they had no clients—instead of worrying about where the next paycheck might come from. They had some household projects to finish, and he was hoping they'd take a day trip somewhere, either inland toward Saint-Paul-de-Vence and the museum there, or along the coast in the direction of Saint-Tropez.

He showered after Liam and then settled down on the king-size bed to relax and catch up on his reading. It was two o'clock before he turned on his computer and logged into his e-mail account. There was a message with a red exclamation mark waiting for him, from his cousin Ellen. It was date-stamped an hour before, and the heading read, *Need your help urgently!*

He clicked it open.

Dear Aidan,

You work for some kind of security company, don't you? My cousin in Turkey is in big trouble and needs help. Can you Skype me? I'll be online till late tonight.

She included her Skype address at the end, with the word *please* followed by multiple exclamation marks.

He looked at the clock and calculated. Nice was five hours ahead of New Jersey, where Ellen lived, so it should be about nine in the morning there. He turned on the webcam, initialized the software, and then connected to Ellen's account.

It took a minute or so before the call went through, and Ellen's face appeared on the screen in front of him. "Hey, cuz," he said. "What's the emergency?"

"I'm so glad you called, Aidan." Over her shoulder she yelled, "Mom! I have Aidan on the computer!"

She turned back to him. "Did you meet my mom's oldest sister, Aunt Eda, when she was here when we were kids?"

It was such an odd question Aidan had to stop and think. "I think so. Is something wrong with her?"

"Not her, my cousin Yahya," she said. "He and his family still live in Istanbul, where my mom was born. Someone has been threatening them."

Aidan's Aunt Sophia appeared in the background of the shot. "See, there's Aidan," Ellen said, pointing.

"His picture?" Aunt Sophia said. "But it's moving!"

"It's live, Mom," Ellen said in the exasperated way of children dealing with parents. "He's in France, remember? And he works for a security company." She looked at Aidan. "Tell her what you do."

"We call it close protection. My partner and I work for a company here in France. They send us out to clients who need bodyguards."

Ellen turned to her mother. "See, I told you! It's perfect!"

"What's perfect?" Aidan asked. "And what kind of threats has your cousin gotten?"

"You tell him, Mom." Ellen jostled her mother so Aidan's aunt's face filled the screen. From behind her, Aidan heard Ellen say, "Just talk."

"Hello, Aidan," Aunt Sophia said. "You look well."

"Mo-om," Ellen said.

"In my own time, Eleni," Aunt Sophia said, using the Turkish diminutive. "Aidan, you remember I have a sister who stayed behind in Turkey when my family came to the US, don't you?"

"Yeah, Ellen was telling me we met her when we were kids."

"That's right. Eda came to visit once with her husband, Victor, maybe twenty years ago."

Aidan sat back in his chair. Their Internet service wasn't measured, and a Skype-to-Skype call was free. So Aunt Sophia could tell whatever story she had at her own pace.

"She was already married, you see, with a baby on the way, when we left," his aunt continued. "Her life has not been easy. She had several miscarriages until she finally had a son, my nephew Yahya."

"Mom, get to the point!" Ellen said from the background.

"Yahya has been very successful," Aunt Sophia said. "All the Abenazos, they have a sense for business. But now Yahya has maybe been too successful. You heard about these problems in Istanbul, with Gezi Park?"

Aidan had noted the news coverage of demonstrations in Istanbul, though he hadn't paid close attention to them. There was so much unrest in the Arab world it was hard to keep track of it all. "Yes. Does your nephew live near there?"

"No, he lives in the old part of the city, near the old shul. But his company was one of the ones supposed to develop the project in Gezi Park. And since then, oh, it has been terrible. My sister is beside herself with worry." She shook her head. "It's always the Jews who get blamed for everything. You know how it is."

Ellen appeared on the screen again, gently pushing her mother out of the way. "I'll take it from here, Mom." She turned to Aidan. "A couple of weeks ago, Yahya got this threatening note, delivered to the doorstep of his house, demanding that he return something. But the note was so garbled he said he couldn't tell what it was the person wanted, or even who it was from."

She picked up a big sports bottle of water and took a long chug. "He ignored it, but then there was another letter, even crazier. Then he was walking down the street near his office, and somebody tried to run him down."

"Was he hurt?"

Ellen shook her head. "But very upset. They don't know what to do, and the police are useless."

"Aren't there private security companies in Istanbul they could hire?"

"I suppose there are. But the whole country is corrupt. You know how things are in those third-world places."

Aidan thought he knew a lot more than Ellen did about living in the third world, but he wasn't going to argue with her.

"Can you and your partner fly to Istanbul and look after Yahya and his family for a week or two?" Ellen asked. "Money won't be a problem. They're rich."

Aidan detected a bit of bitterness in Ellen's voice. As far as he knew, she and her family were comfortably wealthy—big house in the suburbs, fancy cars, kids in private schools. But maybe things weren't as good as he thought. "It's not that simple," Aidan said. "We work for a company. Your cousin would have to call our boss and make the arrangements."

"Give me the information, and I'll get it to Yahya," she said. "His last name is Farias, by the way."

"Are you sure there's no other resource in Turkey?" Aidan asked. "It's going to be very expensive to fly us there and pay the agency, and we have no idea how long the problem will go on."

"If Yahya doesn't want to pay, then he shouldn't have asked for our help," Ellen said.

Aidan told her how Yahya could get hold of Jean-Luc Derain in Marseille. "Thanks, Aidan," Ellen said. "Oh, wait, my mother wants to say good-bye."

Aunt Sophia loomed in front of the camera again. "You'll be careful, Aidan?" she asked.

"Of course," he said. "But really, I doubt we'll end up going there." He ended the call as Liam walked in. "Good, you're home. We may be going out of town soon for a job."

He told Liam about his conversation with his aunt and cousin. "Sounds like a waste of time to me," Liam said. "For us to fly all that way when somebody in Istanbul could handle things."

"That's what I said. This guy may never follow through on calling Jean-Luc."

Liam went to work out in the garden, and Aidan stayed online, refreshing his memory about the incident in Istanbul his aunt had mentioned. Taksim Gezi Park was a small one in the heart of Istanbul, one of the city's few open spaces. The military barracks on the site had been torn down in 1940. Plans had recently been announced to replace the park with a shopping mall and housing.

The people of Turkey had been growing increasingly unhappy with the government's autocratic rule, and as he and Liam had seen in Tunis shortly before they left, that resentment had bubbled up into open protests, using the redevelopment of the park as a focal point. It was bad luck for Yahya Farias to have gotten caught up in that.

Or had the protests simply provided a convenient cover for someone else with a grudge against him?

Aidan had begun to prepare dinner when the phone rang again. "We seem to be awfully busy considering we're not working," he said as he wiped his hands on a towel. He picked up the phone to hear

Jean-Luc's voice.

"So, you are bringing us business now," he said. "This man in Turkey, he is your cousin?"

"Not exactly. My uncle married his aunt. Did he call you?"

"Yes, we had a long conversation. He is a very cultured man, speaks French and English as well as Turkish. He would like to hire you and Liam to protect his family. I assume you will want to take the job?"

"I want to, but I'm not sure about Liam. Let me talk to him and call you back."

"Please do so quickly," Jean-Luc said. "Your cousin is eager to have you there as soon as possible."

Aidan hung up and went out to the garden where Liam had finished his workout and was napping in the shade of a tree, Hayam sprawled at his feet. "Wake up, sleepyhead," Aidan said. "We've been offered a job, if we want to take it."

Liam looked up. "The Al-Nayahans again?"

"No, the job I was telling you about earlier. My cousin's cousin, in Istanbul. He spoke to Jean-Luc, who called a couple of minutes ago."

Liam sat up and stretched. "I don't know, Aidan. It's a long way to go, and we don't know these people or anything about the culture there."

"But they're family," Aidan said.

Liam laughed. "You never even heard of these people till this morning."

"It's not about them. It's about my Aunt Sophia. After my father died, she and my Uncle Harold made sure to invite my mother and me to every family event. And then after my mother was gone too, they said I should think of them as my parents. Uncle Harold died a couple of years ago. Aunt Sophia has never asked anything from me until now."

"Then I guess we're going to Istanbul," Liam said.

4 – Far Enough from Harm

Liam wasn't eager to return to Turkey. The last time he'd been there, for a SEAL operation in the Carpathian Mountains, everything had gone wrong that could have, and his team had lost two good men in an unexpected encounter with Kurdish rebels. Liam had left with a scar on his right calf from a deep knife wound.

But Aidan clearly wanted this assignment, and Liam had long ago accepted that he would do almost anything to make Aidan happy. That in itself was a full-time job, he thought to himself as he began to match up electronic equipment with the appropriate chargers, which had spread all over the apartment.

"I spoke to Jean-Luc and took the job," Aidan said as Liam passed him in the living room, hunting for the charger for Aidan's Kindle. God forbid they ended up somewhere and Aidan had nothing to read. He'd be inconsolable.

"When do we leave?" Liam asked.

"I found a flight that leaves at four p.m. and connects through Paris. We end up in Istanbul just before midnight. I got us one-way tickets since we have no idea how long we'll be staying."

He held up a credit card in his hand. "I love having a card that bills direct to the Agence," he said. "You have to admit, one of the great things about working for them is not having to worry about money."

"I will grant you that," Liam said. Back in Tunis, they'd often had to chase down clients who, once the threat had passed, were unwilling to pay their bills. Now that was the problem of some accountant in Marseille. "You'd better find out if your cousin wants us to come direct to his house when we get in or wait till the morning. With delays and customs, we could be getting to them well after midnight."

"I'll make a note of that," Aidan said.

"I'm going to call Louis and see what he knows about Turkey," Liam said.

Liam had met Louis Fleck when Louis was an attaché at the embassy in Tunis, though that was a cover for his real job with the CIA. He and Louis had become acquaintances, sharing information as appropriate, though Liam had never asked about Louis's personal life. When Aidan entered the picture, he figured out quickly that Louis was gay, which led to a friendship between the two couples: Aidan and Liam, and Louis and his partner, Hassan, a Tunisian architect. Soon after Aidan and Liam relocated to Nice, Louis had accepted a transfer to the consulate there, and Hassan's firm had opened an office in the city as well.

"I promised to get Hassan the address for that guy who repaired your leather vest," Aidan said. "I'll write it down, and you can give it to Louis." On a recent assignment, Liam had torn the seam on his vest, which he loved to wear because it showed off his chest. Aidan had tracked down a leather worker in Vieux Nice who had repaired it.

"Consider me your messenger boy," Liam said, but he smiled

and left Aidan to begin packing their clothes. Aidan was a genius at that; back in Philadelphia, his former partner had traveled a lot for business, and Aidan kept a regular stock of small-sized items for travel. He knew how to fold clothes to minimize wrinkles, what items could do double duty, and a dozen other arcane tips.

In the military, Liam had always packed very light, because he had to hump it all on his back, and he was accustomed to making judgment calls on what to take based on weight and size. Now that his travel was more likely to be by car, plane, or boat than on foot, it was nice to arrive somewhere and discover he had all his own gear around him.

The most important lesson he'd taught Aidan was to pack so that the most necessary items were easily accessible. As a SEAL, that had meant ammunition, bandages and other medical supplies, grenades, mines, a radio, and so on. That also meant putting things in the same place every time—even something as simple as a dopp kit always on the right side at the bottom. Aidan's bag was packed the same way so that in a crisis, either of them could find what they needed in either bag.

They would not be able to take their guns with them; they were not licensed law enforcement, and though there were ways around the situation, they didn't have the time. And Liam's belief was that proper bodyguard procedures kept the client far enough from harm that weapons were not necessary.

Even without firearms, a good bodyguard had to be prepared for many situations. A long-handled mirror could be used to check for bombs under cars. A handheld GPS was useful in unfamiliar locales. Pocketknives, an emergency medical kit, a digital tape recorder and high-quality camera, their laptops, and other computer gear. Not to mention chargers for everything.

He called Louis and made arrangements to meet for a quick coffee at a café a few blocks from the consulate. He dug their hand-cranked radio out of a drawer and turned the crank to be sure the flashlight and cell-phone charger add-ons both worked. Then he found the battery tester and checked all the flashlights and other battery-operated equipment.

He checked that the cigarette lighter had fluid, the matches were dry, and the lightweight parachute cord was still flexible. Binoculars, a loop of wire, a mirror, and a small roll of electrical tape. He remembered a Navy captain who often said, *"There isn't a G-D thing that can't be fixed with a good roll of duct tape."*

When he was finished, he leaned his head in the bedroom door. "I'm going to talk to Louis. Make sure you save something to read on the plane. I'm planning to sleep."

"I downloaded a guidebook to Istanbul," Aidan said. "And don't worry. I've got about fifty unread books on this baby." He held up his Kindle, then put two fingers to his lips and blew Liam a kiss.

Liam mimed catching the kiss in his fist, then turning his hand to send it back to Aidan, who laughed.

As he walked toward the café, Liam thought about the path that had brought them to this sunlit city at the Mediterranean's edge. He would have been happy to stay in the little house behind the Bar

Mamounia in Tunis, accepting only the jobs he wanted, content to have his basic needs taken care of. He didn't need to eat in fancy restaurants, browse in stores with uppity salesclerks, or memorialize every interaction for social media.

Even as he thought that, Liam recognized the positive effect Aidan had on his life. He had opened himself up, not just to love but to friendship and a host of other things. Different sexual positions, different exercise routines, different foods and faces. Liam had been in danger of turning into a hermit back in Tunis, before Aidan stumbled into his life.

He and Aidan were two very different men. Aidan was happiest in cities with fast Internet access and haute cuisine. The French Riviera was perfect for him.

Then why couldn't Aidan be content to stay home? They had plenty of money and didn't have to take this job. But Aidan had some misguided sense of family loyalty as well—this need to remain connected to people who shared his blood. Liam was happy to keep his own family at arm's length.

The café was a small one tucked into the corner of an office building's lobby. Though there was steady takeout traffic, no one ever seemed to stay, so it was a good place for a quiet conversation.

He ordered himself a *café crème*, regular coffee served in a large cup with hot cream. For Louis, a *café noisette*, espresso with a dash of cream in it, called that because of the dark, rich color. With drinks in hand, he settled at a table at the rear of the café and used his cell phone to do some preliminary research on Turkey. He was reading about the Gezi Park protests when Louis slid into the chair across from him.

"You're slipping, McCullough," Louis said as he picked up his coffee. "I could have killed you twelve ways before you'd even have noticed me."

"You paused outside the front door to open it for a Frenchwoman in high heels and a very short skirt," Liam said, putting down his phone. "Four steps into the lobby, you stumbled over the carpet edge. You looked right and left to make sure no one had noticed. Just before you walked into this café, you pulled your cell phone from your pocket and turned off the ringer, then put it away again."

Louis laughed. "I take back everything I said." He sipped his espresso for a moment. "So, you're going to Turkey. Why?"

Liam explained about Aidan's cousin in the US, her cousin in Istanbul, the job through the Agence.

"I didn't know you and Aidan were close to your families," Louis said. "I've never heard either of you mention them."

"It's all this Facebook crap," Liam said. "Suddenly Aidan's whiny about missing stuff back home."

Louis smiled. "You do still call it home."

Liam was determined to get the conversation back on track. "Moving on. Any advice you have for us? We have a plane to catch in a couple of hours."

"The Turkish government is in trouble," Louis said. "A lot of people disagree with Erdogan and his policies, and resentment is bubbling up all over the place. The Gezi Park thing was just so much tinder to the flame."

"You think there's some merit to this cousin's fears?"

"Hard to say without knowing more specifics. Small demonstrations come up, and the police come down on them hard, with tear gas and clubs."

He passed a sheet of paper across the table. "Some contacts that might be useful, some places to avoid, some information from the latest bulletin. Nothing confidential, of course, but I'd keep it close to my vest if I were you."

"That reminds me." Liam handed him the information about the tailor, then looked at his watch. "I'd better get back home. Thanks for meeting me."

He stood and so did Louis. "My pleasure. I suggest you do what you have to do in Turkey and get out as soon as possible. You don't want to get in the middle of what might come down the road."

5 – Bridges

Aidan took Hayam out for a walk and made sure Madame Serroli could take care of her while they were gone. He e-mailed Ellen, letting her know he and Liam were traveling to Istanbul. Then he spent some time online, looking for information about Yahya Farias. Almost everything he could find was in Turkish, and the online translation tools were not exact enough to make much sense. Though Turkish used the Roman alphabet, the words were peppered with cedillas and umlauts, so he had no understanding of how most words were pronounced.

He was worried to learn that Turkish was one of those languages where language was directly connected to social courtesy—second-person pronouns, honorifics, and the T–V distinction, which meant different words and phrasing depending on your level of familiarity with the other person, similar to the *tu* and *vous* in French. Sometimes using the familiar instead of the formal could get you closer to someone—but it could also be insulting.

As a language teacher by training, he was fascinated by such distinctions. He tried to remember if he had ever taught English to a native speaker of Turkish back in Philadelphia. He couldn't recall anyone.

He figured out that Yahya was a past president of business council in Istanbul, and that he was the president of Şirket Farias, or Farias Company. Şirket Farias's business was murky, though Aidan thought that was the fault of the translation software. He couldn't tell if the company built property, or simply owned and rented it. He couldn't find any connection to the project for Gezi Park.

He e-mailed their friend Richard, a British hacker, to see what he could find out about Yahya Farias through unofficial channels, then found a photo of Yahya online. He had a round face like Aidan's Aunt Sophia, black hair, and beetle brows, with a craggy nose.

Liam returned. "What did Louis have to say?" Aidan asked, turning away from the computer.

Liam sat on the sofa, and Hayam hopped up from the floor to nestle in his lap. "He says the situation there is in flux."

"At least that indicates Yahya and his family may have legitimate fears," Aidan said.

"He also gave me some contacts and bulletins. I'll read through them on the plane. You find anything useful?"

"We're going to need visas for Turkey, but we can get them on arrival at our port of entry." He relayed what he'd learned about Yahya, then leaned over to pick up a piece of paper from the coffee table. "I got an e-mail from Ellen with some family information. Aunt Sophia's sister Eda is eighty-eight; Yahya is her second son, who Ellen thinks has to be about sixty. His wife's name is Meryem, and they have two children."

He scanned down the printout. "The older one is named Havva; she's an attorney, graduated from Istanbul University. Ishak is twenty-five, also a college graduate, but Ellen doesn't know what he does for a living." He looked up at Liam. "The good news is that she thinks the whole family, even Aunt Eda, speaks English."

"That will make communication easier," Liam said.

Aidan nodded. "Ellen went to Istanbul to visit them when she was a teenager. They have a large house in a wealthy neighborhood with several servants, and Havva and Ishak are fairly westernized."

"But she didn't have any more idea why somebody wants to kill this cousin or his family?"

"Nope. But Turkey is one of the countries with the widest gap between rich and poor. Along with Chile, Mexico, and the United States. So if these people are wealthy, it could be an economic thing."

"That's easy to deal with in the short term, but if it's an underlying problem, then there isn't much we can do for the long term," Liam said. "We can help them with some general protocols, but we can't protect them for the rest of their lives."

"I know. I figure we'll learn more when we get there. Ellen sent me Yahya's e-mail address, and I sent a note to introduce us, along with when we're getting in. I got an e-mail back that said Yahya will have a car pick us up at the airport and bring us to his house. And that we shouldn't worry about coming in late, because they'll wait for us."

Liam stood. "We've got to leave for the airport in a half hour. You have a cab for us?"

"I'll call for one now," Aidan said. While they waited for the cab, he gathered the perishables from their refrigerator and delivered them, and the dog, to Madame Serroli.

They arrived at the airport in plenty of time for their flight to Paris, and in the departure lounge Aidan opened his Kindle to the

Istanbul guidebook. He read about the magnificent bridge across the Bosporus, one of the engineering marvels of the world, and soon they were on the plane to Paris. The flight was a quick one, and they had only a short layover until they were on the three-and-a-half-hour flight to Istanbul.

Aidan was excited. He always enjoyed this part of an assignment—getting to know the clients and analyzing their situation. This was going to be particularly intriguing, because he had long been fascinated by Aunt Sophia's relatives.

Everyone else in Aidan's family was Ashkenazi—Jews from Russia and Poland who spoke Yiddish with guttural accents and prepared traditional foods like brisket, potato latkes, and kugel. Aunt Sophia was different.

She had grown up in a Sephardic community in Highland Park, New Jersey, a Newark suburb, and her family spoke Ladino at home, the Spanish dialect mixed with Hebrew words. She prepared Mediterranean dishes that fascinated Aidan with their exoticism—fried fish, vegetables stuffed with rice, desserts with dates and apples. Aunt Sophia was the bridge between the two Jewish cultures, and Aidan was always interested in people at that kind of intersection. In a way, he thought, gay men and lesbians performed the same kind of balancing act between their birth families, who were often focused on child-rearing and observing social norms, and their friends, whether single or partnered, social or career-oriented.

Their flight landed at Istanbul Atatürk Airport on time, and they navigated their way to baggage claim and then customs with relative ease. They paid for their visas, had their passports stamped, and then entered the arrival lounge, where a Turkish man in a dark suit held up a sign that read GREENE.

Aidan waved to him, and the man approached them. "Welcome to Istanbul," he said with a heavy accent. "You go to Mr. Farias?"

Aidan nodded. The man took one of the duffels from him and led them to a black car. "We go not far," the driver said as they loaded the trunk. "Maybe ten kilometers."

"Do we cross the Bosporus?" Aidan asked.

The driver shook his head. "No, we go to Balat neighborhood, still on European side."

Aidan did get a view of the magnificent bridge from the highway, though the cabbie exited just before it and drove along the riverfront for a short while, then turned inland. The buildings close to the water were tightly fitted, in a mix of stone and wood painted vibrant colors. As they climbed the gentle slope, though, the houses became larger and more spaced, with trees surrounding them.

The cab pulled into a curving driveway before a two-story stone house with a green roof and overhanging eaves. It reminded Aidan of the architecture of Frank Lloyd Wright in its low, land-hugging lines. The outside lights clicked on with their arrival, and a moment later the front door opened.

Aidan recognized Yahya Farias from his photo. He was shorter than Aidan had expected, slim and well-groomed, with dark hair lacquered in place and an aura of prosperity. Aidan was disappointed that he didn't wear a fez or caftan. "If someone's trying to kill him, it's not too bright to stand in that lit doorway," Liam grumbled as they got out of the cab.

"*Merhaba*," Yahya said and welcomed them both with open arms and led them inside. They left their bags by the door, and Yahya introduced them to the family, who had been waiting for them in the living room.

Aidan's first reaction was that he could have been in his aunt's home in Montclair. The leather sofa with rolled wood arms, the ornate coffee table, even the framed paintings on the walls all could have been shipped direct from New Jersey.

Yahya's mother looked like an older, tinier version of Aunt Sophia. Her round, smiling face was craggier than her younger sister's, and her wispy white hair was cut short instead of in Aunt Sophia's bouffant, but her eyes shone with the same warmth. "*No ay en el mundo amiga komo la madre*," Yahya said as he introduced them. "A Ladino proverb. There is no friend in the world like your mother."

"*Amor kon amor se paga*," his mother said in return. "That is another. When you give love, you are repaid with love." She took both Aidan's hands in hers. "You both must call me *Teyze* Eda. Teyze, it means *aunt* in the Turkish language."

Seeing mother and son together, Aidan was struck by a pang of loss, wishing he could share proverbs with his own mother once again. Sisters-in-law, she and Aunt Sophia had been more like sisters, talking to each other on the phone regularly, alternating holidays between homes.

He looked at the rest of the family as he was introduced to them. Meryem Farias could have fit into any Hadassah meeting—dark hair, elegant posture, gold necklace, and bracelets. Both Havva and Ishak were taller than their parents, slim and willowy. They could have almost been twins, and both wore well-tailored Western-style clothing.

Teyze Eda excused herself to go to bed, and Aidan realized it was very late. "We must have a toast to your arrival!" Yahya said. "And then in the morning we will talk."

He brought out a bottle of raki—an anise-flavored brandy that Aidan knew was a specialty of the country; he'd taken a bartending course back in Philadelphia to be able to mix perfect cocktails for his ex-partner Blake's business contacts. Meryem removed a set of glass cups covered in silver filigree from a cabinet, and Yahya poured for each of them, adding a few drops of water from a silver pitcher.

The liquid turned a cloudy white. "We call this *aslan sütü*—lion's milk," Yahya said. "Milk for the strong and courageous. As you both are."

Aidan sipped the liquor, which reminded him of the French drink pastis, a similar licorice-flavored drink served with water on the Riviera.

All in all, the sense of familiarity was odd, even more disorienting than a completely new environment would have been. They chatted about Aidan and Liam's flight and the weather forecast—sunny, in the low seventies, little chance of rain—and then Aidan stifled a yawn, and Yahya said, "We are keeping you awake after your long trip. Please, Ishak will show you to your room."

Ishak rose from the sofa with a kind of languid grace that Aidan immediately recognized. He walked to an archway across the room, and his father said something sharply to him in Turkish. He frowned, then returned to pick up Aidan's duffle bag. "Please, follow me," he said in a poor attempt at manners.

Aidan and Liam grabbed their other bags and followed him down a hallway, past several closed doors. "Do you live here with your parents?" Aidan asked.

"My sister and I lived together in an apartment until recently," he said. "Our parents forced us to return."

Aidan and Liam shared a glance. Aidan thought the boy's resentment didn't bode well for family unity during a difficult time. But perhaps he had been able to live a freer, more open life with his sister and wasn't happy to give that up.

Ishak turned right at the end of the hallway. "This is the original house," he said. "Where my grandparents lived until my *dede*, my grandfather, he died, and my father bought the house next door and tore it down, and built new and connected."

He stopped before a door and opened it. "This will be your room. You only need one bed, I believe?" There was no sense of kinship in the words, or in his face, which Aidan found curious.

Someone had told Yahya they were gay. Jean-Luc? Ellen? It didn't appear to be a problem for the Fariases.

"That's fine," Aidan said. He stepped into the room, furnished with a large bed of ornately carved wood, with matching tables and bureau.

"Gizem, she is the maid. She makes the breakfast at nine," Ishak said. "You will go back the way we came. Good night."

He turned and left them. "Not a real charmer, is he?" Liam said after he'd shut the bedroom door.

"How would you feel if you had to move back in with your parents in your twenties?" Aidan said as he hoisted his duffle onto the bed. "Especially being gay."

"Did you notice how smooth his skin is? Probably a cross-dresser."

Aidan was surprised. Liam wasn't usually so perceptive when it came to identifying other gay people. "What?" Liam said in response to his look. "You think you're the only one with gaydar?"

"You continue to surprise me." Aidan yawned again. "But we'd better get to sleep if we're going to be any use tomorrow."

"That assumes there's something we can do," Liam grumbled.

6 — Wake-Up Call

Liam was a man of routines. Though they'd gone to bed very late, he still woke at seven. Aidan rolled over and went back to sleep, but Liam got up and found his way out to the garden to exercise.

He warmed up with a dozen sun salutations, then did a hundred push-ups and a hundred sit-ups. He had the sense that someone was watching him, but he continued his exercises. When he had finished his jumping jacks and leg stretches, a glass door slid open, and Ishak stepped outside, carrying two mugs of coffee.

"Good morning, Liam *Bey*," he said. "You would like?"

"Thanks," Liam said, taking the mug from him. Their fingers grazed as he did, but neither of them remarked on it. They sat at a wrought-iron table beside a vine-draped pergola. The sun passed intricate patterns onto the pavement in front of them.

Liam remembered from the brief dossier Aidan had compiled that they didn't know what Ishak did for a living, so as they drank, he asked.

"There are two answers to that question," Ishak said, looking at him. "The truth, and what my parents believe."

"Let's start with the truth," Liam said. "Nothing you tell me or Aidan will go back to your parents unless it involves keeping you all safe."

"Until Havva and I were forced to return here, I worked at a restaurant," Ishak said. "I was a hostess there."

Liam doubted that the gender-changed pronoun was a mistake. "A special kind of restaurant, I assume," Liam said.

"That is true."

Effeminate men made Liam uncomfortable. He'd never done drag himself, or dated anyone who did, and if Aidan had ever suggested it, Liam would have vetoed it quickly. But Ishak didn't bother him in the same way. He was more gender neutral than effeminate, and he and his sister seemed almost interchangeable.

"And Havva? Is she…"

"Like me, my sister prefers to wear women's clothes." Ishak looked Liam in the eye. "And like me, she prefers to share her bed with a man."

"Then we all have something in common," Liam said. "Not the clothes, but the choice of bed partners." He drank the rest of the coffee, which was strong and sweet.

"There are others like Aidan Bey in our family?" Ishak asked.

"You'd have to ask him that," Liam said. "You and your family are the first of his relatives I've met."

"But cousin Ellen, she knows of you and Aidan."

That answered one of Liam's questions. It had been Aidan's nosy cousin. But it was what it was. "Only through Aidan," he said.

"You will wish to shower before breakfast." Ishak extended his hand, and Liam gave him the empty mug. Ishak stood and smiled. "And thank you for the performance this morning. It was most stimulating."

That creeped Liam out. Yeah, Aidan had often said he was an

exhibitionist, because he preferred to work out in the nude when he could and didn't mind admiring glances. But glances were one thing; "stimulation" was another.

He went back into the bedroom, where Aidan was stirring. "Get up, sleepyhead," Liam said. "I'm taking a shower; then it's your turn."

Aidan yawned, and Liam went into the bathroom, doubting his partner would still be awake when he finished his shower.

No surprise; when he went back into the bedroom, drying off with a large, fluffy towel, he saw Aidan was asleep again. He walked over to him and positioned his dick in front of his partner's mouth. He draped the damp towel over his shoulders and thought of slim, willowy Ishak, who reminded him of Abdullah, a queeny guy he'd fooled around with in Tunis, before Aidan. His dick stiffened, and he waited patiently for Aidan to realize he was standing there.

"Really, Liam?" Aidan said, his eyes still closed.

"Really what?"

"You think I don't know where you are? Or where your dick is?"

"Hey, I'm just drying off after my shower," Liam said. "Wondering when you're going to get up."

Aidan opened his eyes and smiled. "Whereas you're already up." He reached out and grasped the base of Liam's dick and pulled it closer to his mouth. Liam shivered at the touch, and the way Aidan used his middle finger to stroke Liam's perineum.

Aidan took him in his mouth. Liam sighed deeply as Aidan swallowed him and then began a gentle sucking, still stroking his balls and perineum. Liam gulped as he felt enveloped in that soft wetness, and he reached out to stroke Aidan's head.

Quickly, though, he pushed toward Aidan, pumping his dick in and out of Aidan's mouth, his fingers clenched around a hank of Aidan's hair. As his orgasm rose, he panted and stifled a whimper, and then he ejaculated down Aidan's throat.

Aidan swiped his tongue up and down Liam's shaft, then pulled back. "That was a nice wake-up call."

"I had a wake-up of my own, with Ishak," Liam said. "Which I'll tell you all about once you get dressed."

"Liam!"

"You heard me. Get your cute butt into the shower."

While Aidan showered, Liam dressed in his regular jockstrap, khaki slacks, and black Agence polo shirt. Then he unpacked the gear he'd brought, verifying that everything was ready for use.

Aidan stepped out of the shower, toweling his hair, and Liam took in the sight for a moment. Aidan was much more muscular than he'd been when they first met, though the fine dark hair over his arms and legs camouflaged that. His waist was slim and his stomach flat, without Liam's definition.

His smile was all Aidan, and just as charming as it had been two years before. No wonder someone like Ishak made so little impression on him, when he had Aidan.

Aidan pulled a pair of boxers from the bureau drawer. "So? Ishak?" he asked as he stepped into them.

"He was watching me exercise this morning," Liam said. "I was right. Until his parents summoned him back here, he was working as a 'hostess' at a gay bar."

"He didn't make a pass at you, did he?"

"More an acknowledgment than a pass," Liam said. "Don't go getting jealous. He's your cousin."

"He's my cousin's cousin. No real relation to me."

"You know the kind of man I like," Liam said. "A man, not someone who sits on the fence halfway between male and female."

Aidan finished getting dressed, and they walked down the hall to the kitchen, where Ishak sat across from his father. "Good, you are here," Yahya said. "I must go into my office this morning. You will come with me?"

"I'll go," Liam said. "Aidan, you can stay here and get to know your family."

"Good, good," Yahya said. "We will leave in half an hour."

They ate a breakfast of fresh bread, fruit, and juice. Then Liam met Yahya in the garage, where they climbed into Yahya's SUV. Yahya carried a leather satchel the size of a woman's small handbag. "Your briefcase?" Liam asked.

"I have begun carrying all my family's important papers with me," Yahya said. "I prefer to have them close rather than locked up somewhere."

"Tell me more about what happened to you," Liam asked as Yahya backed out of the garage.

"It started with a letter," he said. "Now I wish I had kept it, but at the time I thought it was nonsense."

"What kind of a letter?"

"Badly written and rambling. This person, whoever he is, demanded that I turn something over that belonged to him."

As Yahya drove down the hill from his home and entered a maze of small streets, Liam asked, "You don't know who sent the letter?"

Yahya shook his head. "And I don't know what this thing is that he wants. You see why I threw the letter away."

"Written in what language?"

"Turkish. But very bad writing, almost insulting."

Liam looked over at him as Yahya made a sharp turn from one narrow street to another. "Insulting in what way?"

Yahya shrugged. "Hard to say. Maybe it was the way he wrote, not like a letter but a demand, or maybe just the words."

"And when was this?"

"I have been trying to remember," Yahya said. "I think it was perhaps two months ago, maybe more."

"Did this person ever follow up?"

They stopped at a traffic light, and an endless stream of pedestrians crossed in front of them. Istanbul was a very congested city, and Liam wondered why anyone would live there who could afford to live elsewhere.

"At first, no," Yahya said when the light changed, and he began to inch into the intersection, forcing the pedestrians to hurry forward or backward. "Maybe one month later there was another letter. This one said that it was my daughter who had stolen this thing. But when I showed it to her, she denied any knowledge. We could not understand why someone who felt Havva had done something against him would have come to me instead of to her."

"So you ignored it again?"

Yahya nodded. The sleeves of his Western-style business suit bunched up as he clenched his hands around the steering wheel. "She graduated from law school. Until recently she worked for an attorney we know through our shul."

For a moment Liam thought Yahya's accent had gotten in the way of the word *school*, but then he remembered Aidan often used the Yiddish word *shul* to mean his synagogue.

"This other attorney, he didn't know anything either?"

"You have to understand, these letters were written by someone who was almost illiterate. He did not even spell Havva's name correctly."

"Any letters after that?"

"No. But there were two more things, which now I believe were connected. Maybe three weeks after the second letter, someone broke into our house while we were all out. Many things were moved around, closets and drawers opened, but nothing valuable was stolen, as far as we could tell. Only copies of some official papers to do with travel. But it is possible that they were lost, not stolen."

"Let me guess," Liam said. "You didn't call the police."

"To tell them what? They would have laughed at us." He shook his head. "Then last week, I was walking down the street near my office, and a crazy-looking man in a very old Japanese car tried to run me over."

Liam wasn't sure about that. He'd seen the way Yahya drove, and the other drivers around him, and it could have been an unconnected incident.

"That is when my mother became very frightened. She spoke with her sister in America, who told us about you."

"You didn't report that either?"

"Ha! The police here, they are corrupt. And you forget, we are Jews."

"What does that have to do with it?"

"We are such a small minority here in Turkey. And there is a long history, you know, of blaming every problem on the Jews."

Yahya turned into the parking lot for a four-story office building and pulled into a spot with a numbered sign. "This your regular spot?" Liam asked.

"Yes."

"You might need to park somewhere else," Liam said, remembering a client whose car had been rigged with a bomb when it was parked where expected.

"We will not be here that much longer," Yahya said as he unbuckled his seat belt.

"What do you mean?"

"No one has told you? My family is preparing to leave Istanbul. We will join my cousins in the United States. The missing papers were copies of the documents we have been working on for some time—our visas and work permits. Fortunately they were only copies, so we will be able to leave here very soon."

7 – Jewish History

After Liam and Yahya left, Aidan remained in the kitchen with Ishak, both of them lingering over their coffee. Meryem and Havva joined them a few minutes later. He was amused to see both mother and daughter eat Western-style cereal with milk and sliced banana. So much for exotic cuisine.

"Have you always lived here in Istanbul?" Aidan asked Meryem as she sipped her coffee.

"We come from a long line of Jews who left Spain during the Inquisition," she said. "Most of them have lived in Turkey for many generations. Only my mother, Evadne, came here from Greece, to marry my father."

"Greece?"

She nodded. "A town called Ioannina. My father, Jacobo, went there for trading and fell in love with my mother in 1940. Her father opposed the marriage, so they eloped, coming back here to my grandfather's home."

"He opposed?" Aidan asked. "Why? Because your grandfather was Jewish?"

"Oh no. We are all Jews. My mother never said, but I think it was because my grandfather was the rabbi, and he felt my father wasn't good enough for her." She stood and began to collect the empty coffee cups. "It was very lucky for her, because soon the Nazis came in and sent most of the people of the town to the camps. Only my mother's youngest brother survived."

"That's terrible," Aidan said. "My family was lucky. My great-grandparents left Lithuania and Russia in the early 1900s for the US."

"It seems we Jews can never live in the same place for too long," Meryem said sadly. "Whenever there are problems, it is the Jews who are to blame."

"Is that the case here?" Aidan asked. "Is there anti-Jewish feeling?"

"Many Muslims I have met do not like Jews," Havva said. "Despite the fact that we come from the same origins and even share many beliefs. Kemal Atatürk, the founder of modern Turkey, was determined to make this a secular country, to control the radical elements of Islam. But there are many today who would destroy his legacy."

"You're an attorney, aren't you?" Aidan asked.

She nodded. "My specialty is international trade, particularly with America."

"No wonder your English is so good."

"We all study English from a very young age," Ishak said.

Meryem finished the cleanup. "I have many details to accomplish," she said. "Is there anything we can provide for you, Aidan?"

"No, thank you. Will you all be staying home this morning?"

The three of them agreed.

"Then I don't need anything more than access to your Internet."

Ishak accompanied him back to the room he shared with Liam,

and provided the access code for the house's Wi-Fi. "How is it in America for people like you and me?" he asked.

Aidan sighed as the laptop began to connect to the Internet. "It's not as good as it could be. And it depends on where you are. The big cities? Mostly they are very accepting. In many states now, two men, or two women, can marry each other. There are rules in place to prevent bullying, and courses to educate people. But there is still a lot to be done."

He looked at Ishak, who sat on the edge of the bed. "How is it here?"

"It is something we do not talk of. The laws against our behaviors have been repealed, but that does not mean it is always safe for us. We are still a very conservative country. And like you say of the US, it is better in the cities than in the countryside. You know we have mandatory military service?"

"I didn't." Aidan couldn't imagine the delicate Ishak serving in the army. "Have you served?"

Ishak smiled. "The military does not believe that homosexuals can be good soldiers. I have been excused."

"So your parents know about you?"

He shook his head. "They believe I am still covered by my student deferment." He stood. "I will see you for lunch."

As Aidan accessed his e-mail, he was grateful again for the opportunities provided him by his great-grandparents. He could only imagine how difficult it must have been for them, to leave behind family, country, and language to make new lives in an unfamiliar land, all in the hope that the future would be better for their children and grandchildren.

He dealt with most of the e-mail quickly, saving the message from Richard in England for last. Their hacker friend had attached a short report on Yahya Farias and family, with a promise of more to come.

Aidan opened it and began to read. Richard had not been able to discover any connection between Yahya or his company and the Gezi Park project. That was curious; Aidan was sure Aunt Sophia had mentioned it, even citing it as a reason why someone would want to threaten Yahya.

A great deal of financial detail followed. For the past several years, Yahya had been selling assets in Turkey and transferring the funds overseas. Much of the money had gone into accounts in tax havens like Switzerland and the Cayman Islands. Richard noted that it would be an extra charge for him to obtain information there, due to the secrecy involved.

It was clear that Yahya Farias was very wealthy, and that he had been planning an exit strategy from Turkey for quite some time. Why? Had he received other threats over the years? Were these last attempts on his life a culmination of a longer process?

Aidan wished Liam was there to discuss these questions. Liam had not returned by lunch, however, and Aidan joined Meryem, Havva, and Ishak in the dining room, where they were served by the maid.

"Where do you live in America?" Havva asked.

"We don't live in the States," Aidan said. "We're based in Nice right now, but before that Liam lived in Tunis. I was there with him for two years."

"Why don't you live in America if you can? I would love to live there. Turkey is so backward."

"I've always wanted to live overseas," Aidan said. "After graduate school I spent two years teaching in Europe. I only went back home for a visit, but then I fell in love and stayed there. When I had a chance to travel again, I took it."

That was a pretty quick summary of his life, Aidan thought. But it was all they needed to know for right now. He turned to Meryem. "What can you tell me about these threats you have experienced?"

"Threats?" Meryem asked.

"He means the stupid letters," Havva said. "Some illiterate person sent us a few letters demanding that I return something I stole from him. But I have never stolen anything in my life. And he never even said who he was, or what it was he thought I had stolen from him."

"Could it have been related to your job?" Aidan asked.

Havva shook her head. "I worked for a lawyer since I left law school. But only in his office, doing research, and never with clients. I never took anything from one of them."

"This is boring," Ishak said. "Aidan, please tell us about where our cousins live. It is very nice?"

Aidan nodded. His father's brother, Uncle Harold, had made a lot of money in the wholesale jewelry business in New York, and

Aidan had many memories of extravagant bat mitzvahs and weddings, holiday dinners at restaurants with singing waiters. "When I was growing up, they lived in Teaneck—a town outside New York City."

Ishak sighed. "New York."

"Uncle Harold worked there, in the jewelry district around Canal Street. He died a couple of years ago—just before I left the States." Aidan remembered Blake's unwillingness to accompany him to his uncle's funeral. Was that a sign of what would grow into a larger problem?

He shook that thought off. "Ellen and Jessica were already married, so Aunt Sophia sold the big house and moved to a condo overlooking the Hudson River and the New York skyline."

He hadn't been there; his aunt's move had taken place when he was already in Tunisia. But he'd seen pictures.

"Ellen and Jessica?" Havva asked. "Where do they live?"

"Ellen is married and has two children. Her son's bar mitzvah was last month. They live a few miles from Aunt Sophia. Jessica moved to California after college, and she and her husband live there."

"Hollywood?" Ishak asked hopefully.

Aidan shook his head. "Silicon Valley. Outside San Francisco. They both work in the software business. No children."

"We will meet them all?" Havva asked.

"I don't know," Aidan said. "Are you planning to visit the US?"

The maid came in to clear the dishes, and it was only when she left that Meryem spoke again. "Visit? We are moving there. It has been a process of some time—gaining the sponsorship of my husband's aunt and cousin, applying for visas and work permits, and making an investment in the United States. That is why you are here, is it not? To help us with this relocation?"

Aidan couldn't hide his surprise. "I think we've had some crossed wires," he said. "Misunderstanding. Liam and I are bodyguards—we protect people from threats. We were told someone had tried to kill you, and you needed our protection."

"This is very strange," Meryem said. "Yes, we have received these letters. And my husband, once he felt that someone in a car tried to hit him. But you must understand how the people drive here in Istanbul."

Aidan didn't like being kept in the dark. What was Yahya Farias up to? Was there really a threat? And if so, from whom, and toward which family member? Aidan wanted to talk to Liam and let him know what Meryem had said. Maybe together they could figure out what was going on.

Meryem looked at the clock and said, "I must hurry. I will have my hair prepared for a dinner this evening."

"You're going out?" Aidan asked.

"Yahya and I are patrons of a Jewish charity here in Istanbul. Tonight is the fund-raising dinner."

"I don't think you should go out to such a public place while your family is being threatened," Aidan said.

"You do not understand. This is a farewell to us, because we are leaving, so we must go. And I don't believe in these threats you speak of anyway."

"I should come with you to the hairdresser," he said. "To be careful."

Meryem laughed. "It is a silly appointment."

He insisted, and after gaining reassurance from Havva and Ishak that they would stay with their grandmother at the house while he and Liam were both gone, Aidan accompanied Meryem. She was dressed casually, in midcalf pants his mother would have called pedal pushers, a blouse in a bright-colored abstract print, and several gold chains. She carried a large expensive handbag.

Her car was a small, sporty convertible, and she navigated the narrow streets with ease. The salon, called Les Femmes, was on a side street a mile or so from the house. Meryem pulled the car into a parking space and led him inside. It looked a lot like any beauty parlor anywhere—rows of barber chairs and mirrored counters, a tile floor of black and white diamonds, photos of hairstyles posted on the walls.

While Meryem had her hair done, he sat in the lobby, trying to read more of the guidebook to Istanbul. But he couldn't concentrate; he kept thinking about the Fariases.

He felt very connected to them, even though he'd known them for less than twenty-four hours. Was it a Jewish thing—that they shared the same religion? Back home, he'd often connected with someone quickly, not knowing his or her religion, then discovered the shared heritage.

It was part of what he'd heard called Jewish radar. The ability, or need, to identify people who shared your religion, cultivated over centuries of persecution and life in exile. When he looked back at his childhood, he recognized that most of his earliest friends were kids from his own neighborhood, thrown together by an accident of geography. Once he began elementary school and Sunday school, however, he gravitated toward the other Jewish kids.

Was it just that they were together six days a week, rather than the five of their public-school classmates? Or something deeper? He had grown up in a secular world, always conscious of being one of a small number of Jews at his school, in his neighborhood, in his town. That fact had been drilled into him in Sunday school and Hebrew school, as his teachers reinforced his cultural uniqueness but also his people's isolation from their neighbors. *"Look at the German Jews,"* he had been taught. *"They thought they were German, until the Nazis took over."*

His first experience of being less isolated came when he was a freshman at the University of Pennsylvania. A walk down his dormitory hallway revealed Jewish names on almost every other door, often accompanied by mezuzahs—the tiny encased scrolls posted on Jewish doorposts. His friends ate at the campus Hillel, wore yarmulkes and kept kosher, and exposed him to beliefs and habits he'd never known, like not wearing leather shoes on the High Holidays.

He had embraced all that religion, desperate for a sense of belonging to something larger. He had been brought up in the

Reform tradition, but he began to attend Conservative and Orthodox services with his friends. Coming out of the closet, though, had derailed that.

Some Orthodox friends felt homosexuality was a choice, and a sin. Some of his gay friends had no religion at all, and Aidan felt odd talking about beliefs with them. He'd taken off after graduate school to travel and teach, then landed with Blake Chennault, who had no religious beliefs whatsoever and didn't encourage Aidan either.

When his parents died, he had observed all the rituals, and each year he tried to find a synagogue on the anniversaries of their deaths, to say the Kaddish prayer. Liam, a lapsed Catholic, found his beliefs interesting and somewhat exotic, never discouraging him, but also never seeking to join him.

It wasn't a sticking point between them, but still Aidan worried. Before they knew he was gay, his parents had pressured him to have Jewish friends, date Jewish girls. It had been a family scandal when one of his cousins married a Christian woman. His parents had often said relationships were difficult enough without bringing in extra tensions based on different backgrounds.

The front door to the salon jangled open, and Aidan looked up. The young man in the doorway didn't look like a client of Les Femmes—especially as his head was completely shaved. He wore a pair of tattered blue jeans and a black T-shirt with an image of a mustachioed skull wearing a fez, with the slogan *Young Turks* in white.

In a matter of seconds, the room was silent, all eyes on the man in the doorway.

8 – Responsibility

Aidan looked around the salon. Meryem was in a good position, toward the rear of the large room, facing a mirror. The middle-aged female stylist was about halfway through working a complicated braid into Meryem's hair.

The man said something in Turkish, and Aidan sensed the mood in the salon relax, though he had no idea what had been said. The man turned and walked back out, letting the glass door slam behind him.

The women in the salon resumed their chatter, and Aidan walked over to where Meryem sat. "What did that man say?"

"His mother was sick and cannot come for her hair appointment." She looked up at him. "Why?"

"It's awkward protecting someone where you don't understand the language. You have to rely on your instincts, on body language, and on tone of voice."

She nodded. "And you thought this man might want to hurt me?"

"It's what we're here for," he said.

He went back to his seat, wondering again why he felt so connected to the Fariases. Was it a feeling of family? Though there was no blood between him and these people, Teyze Eda looked and acted a lot like his Aunt Sophia, her younger sister. Yahya reminded him of his father; he was a mensch, the Yiddish word for *man*, which carried with it a connotation of being a good person who looked out for his family and community.

In any case, he did feel connected to them. He often empathized with clients and came to care about them as people, but there was something different here—a much deeper, quicker connection.

It wasn't something he could talk to Liam about. Liam preferred to remain all business when it came to clients—to avoid emotional entanglements that might get in the way of his job. It was one of the biggest, most profound differences between them, and one that Aidan often felt he had to skate around.

He kept his gaze on the front door and was relieved when Meryem was finished. He hovered behind her as she gave her credit card to the clerk, then looked both ways outside before opening the door for Meryem. A blast of warm, humid air hit them.

"You look lovely," he said, and it was true. Her auburn hair had been coiled artfully around her head, and she looked elegant. He watched around them as they walked to the car, and waited while Meryem lowered herself carefully inside. He closed the door behind her, then got in. They were quiet for most of the ride back to the house. Trying to lighten the mood, Aidan asked, "You and Yahya Bey are very involved in charity work here in Istanbul?"

"As Jews, we have the responsibility to look after our own. In my family, it begins with my uncle Nissim. When he came to Istanbul after the camps, he was a boy of fourteen with nothing. My parents gave him food and clothing and arranged for him to learn a trade."

Aidan listened while at the same time keeping an eye on the

street around them. He couldn't shake the feeling that despite the family's blasé attitude, there was a real threat out there. But everyone appeared occupied with their own affairs. Many tourists looked fresh off a cruise ship, and even the Turkish locals were dressed Western-style.

"From that experience, my parents began to do charitable works. First with refugees from the war, then with poor Jews here. They always said '*Aze kon el prove, y el Dyo te pagara.*' Do with the poor, and the Lord will repay you." She pulled away from the curb and darted into the flow of traffic, ignoring the horns blasting behind her.

"And your uncle? What happened to him?"

Meryem sighed. "That is very sad. He has always been a bitter man, unhappy with what life brings him. He refused to go to school or take the apprenticeship my father arranged. He went to work at the docks, married a Greek woman, and estranged himself. The only time my family ever hears from him is when he needs money."

When they returned to the house, he found Liam already in their room. "I had a very interesting morning with the family," Aidan said.

"Mine with Yahya was pretty interesting too. Or confusing." Liam told him about Yahya's intention to leave Turkey.

Aidan confirmed it based on his conversation with Meryem. "She believes that's why we're here—to help them with the move."

"Help them how?" Liam asked.

"I don't know. I'm just telling you what she said. And there's more. According to what Richard dug up, this move has been in the works for a long time."

"What do you mean?"

"Let me show you the dossier he sent." They looked it over again, together. "Yahya has been selling property in Turkey and salting the money away overseas for a couple of years. He made some major investments in US real estate. Along with the sponsorship of his aunt and his cousin, those qualified him and his family for one of those investment-based visas."

Liam sat back against the bed pillows. "What's going on here?" he asked. "Were there really any attempts on Yahya's life? He doesn't have any of those threatening letters. Why are we here, if there haven't been, and they're picking up to move to the States?"

"And why doesn't anyone seem frightened?" Aidan asked. "Did Yahya tell you about this big dinner they're going to tonight?"

"Yup. I tried to convince him to skip it, but he insisted."

"I did the same with Meryem. How do you want to handle things, then?"

"One of us should go with them, the other one stay here," Liam said.

"If Havva and Ishak agree to stay here, then we could both go," Aidan said. "A big event like this, with their names listed as patrons, would be a good opportunity for someone to go after them. It would be better to have both of us."

Aidan was glad that he had packed one set of dress clothes for each of them—black slacks in a linen-polyester blend that didn't wrinkle, tan cotton shirts he'd bought back in Tunis, embroidered with swirling patterns, and black loafers. It was the kind of outfit that would fit in at a variety of locations without standing out. He wished for a moment that he'd brought the gold bracelet Liam had bought him for their first anniversary—it would have looked great with the outfit.

"Earth to Aidan," Liam said.

Aidan turned away from his reflection in the mirror. "Sorry, I was daydreaming."

"I know. You do that a lot."

Aidan frowned. "Did you need something?"

"It's time to take this show on the road, even though that's a stupid idea."

They walked out of the house as the sun was setting, and the skyline was filled with the dark silhouettes of mosques, their domes and spires creating a mural against the lavender clouds.

Yahya drove, with Liam in the front seat beside him, and Meryem and Aidan in the back. The affair was being held at one of the modern high-rise hotels near Taksim Square in downtown Istanbul, and Yahya left the car with a valet at the entrance. He took Meryem's hand, and they walked forward, with Aidan and Liam following.

In the lobby they passed huge windows overlooking the Bosporus and the Golden Horn, and the cityscape shone brilliantly. Aidan saw the glowing dome of the Hagia Sophia Mosque and its surrounding minarets and experienced a pang of disappointment that it didn't look like they were going to see much of Istanbul at all.

They entered a large banquet hall with glittering chandeliers and twenty-some round tables. Yahya and Meryem kissed and hugged almost everyone they encountered. A giant banner hung at one end of the room in Turkish and Hebrew, and though Aidan could sound out the Hebrew words, he had little idea what they meant.

Aidan was a bit surprised to see that other guests had personal protection too. He and Liam conferred with four other guards in a mix of Arabic and fractured English, and they each took stations around the room, as close to their principals as possible.

The whole affair was conducted in Turkish, so Aidan had no idea what was going on. There were speeches, then dinner service and more speeches. His stomach grumbled, though he had no expectation of being fed. He couldn't understand a word of what was spoken, but it appeared the hosts of each table were thanked for their contributions. People stood and were applauded.

He leaned back against the wall and thought about the Fariases. He should have called Ellen as soon as he got that report from Richard. Tried to find out anything else she might know about her cousins. Aunt Sophia had clearly helped with their sponsorships.

He glanced at his watch as servers began to deliver coffee and dessert, and he prayed the evening would end soon. It was already ten o'clock, and there were still a number of tables yet to be introduced.

He was watching Meryem and Yahya drink their coffee when he saw her reach for her small, gilded purse. She retrieved her cell phone and put it to her ear, covering her other ear with her hand.

Then she spoke to Yahya, and they both stood. They appeared to be making apologies to their guests, and Aidan caught Liam's eye and nodded toward them. They met the Fariases at the door to the ballroom.

"Is something wrong?" Aidan asked.

"Havva and Ishak," Meryem said, her voice catching. "They have been attacked."

9 – Variations

Liam asked, "They were attacked at the house?" He was angry at himself for allowing the family to be separated. He should have insisted that either they remain together, or they hire additional security.

"No, they were near here," Meryem said. "Havva did not say exactly where, just that they were in Beyoglu, and that she had gone to the hospital with Ishak."

"How is he?" Aidan asked.

Liam knew that was the appropriate question to ask, but he was more interested in where the two had been, and why they hadn't remained at home as they had promised.

"Havva believes his arm has been broken," Meryem said.

Yahya didn't want to wait for his car, or worry about parking at the hospital, so he had the doorman hail him a cab. The four of them squeezed inside. Liam had no opportunity to talk to Aidan, and he realized, not for the first time, how important it had become to him to be part of a couple, a team.

Despite the late hour, there was a lot of traffic, and the atmosphere in the taxi was anxious. After what seemed like a long time, but was probably only about ten minutes, they were at the hospital's brightly lit emergency entrance, with the word *ACIL* in white block letters against a red background.

When they walked in, the room was empty except for an elderly man who moaned quietly, a young man doubled over in what looked like stomach pain, and a family with a young girl, her arm wrapped in makeshift bandages.

Across the room he saw Havva on a hard plastic chair beside a very attractive woman of about her age, with shoulder-length brown hair and careful makeup. She wore a long red silk dress, marred only by the white cast on her right arm.

It took Liam an extra beat to recognize that was Ishak in the red dress.

Ishak's parents appeared to take that long as well. Meryem rushed over to him, speaking rapidly in Turkish. He looked down and mumbled a reply. She sat on the other side of him, still talking. His sister took his good hand and looked defiantly toward her father, Aidan, and Liam.

Yahya stood in the doorway, and the sliding glass doors opened and closed behind him. Liam had seen that look of shock on men in combat. "I must return to the hotel to retrieve my car," Yahya said to Liam. "You will come with me?"

Liam nodded. "We'll come back here?"

"My wife can secure a taxi to the house," Yahya said and strode out of the emergency room. Liam had time to share only a glance with his partner before he had to follow the client out the door.

Yahya was silent in the cab ride, though Liam could tell the man was full of conflicting emotions. When they were back in Yahya's car on the way home, Liam could bear the silence no longer. He said, "I've broken my arm twice. As long as it's not a serious break, Ishak should be fine in about six weeks."

Yahya didn't answer. Liam hated the way the evening had turned out—he felt responsible for Ishak's injury, even though the boy had promised to stay home. This kind of personal conversation with a client was much more Aidan's purview. His partner had the ability to empathize with clients, to get them to open up and talk to him.

And Liam was hungry. As a SEAL he'd gone without food for a day or more, but he was older now, and all the easy living on the Riviera had made him soft. He looked forward to his regular meals.

"Did you know this?" Yahya asked.

Liam wasn't sure what Yahya meant, and he knew that whatever he said, he'd screw up somehow. But he had to plunge ahead, no matter how uncomfortable it made him.

"Aidan has often told me about this thing he calls Jewish radar," he said. "How he can meet a stranger and immediately tell the other person is Jewish. Does that happen to you too?"

Yahya gripped the steering wheel, but he nodded. "I believe it comes from centuries of oppression of our people. We gained an ability to recognize people like us quickly, to know if we could be safe."

"That's it," Liam said. "Aidan also says there's a similar thing with gay people. That we recognize our own, on some intuitive level."

"And you saw this in my son?"

"I'm not sure what we saw," Liam said. "And I refuse to make judgments about anyone until I have concrete evidence. But yes, there was a connection. And this morning, Ishak watched me while I exercised. We talked."

Yahya looked over at him.

"Just a very quick conversation. But he asked how things are for…" Liam hesitated. "For people like Aidan and me, in America."

"So you also wear women's clothes?" Yahya asked.

Liam suppressed a shudder. "I think there are many different variations in people," he said carefully. He hated to reveal anything of his personal life to a client, but in this case he couldn't help it. "There are men, like Aidan and me, who prefer to be with other men. But neither of us wishes to be a woman, or to dress like one."

Yahya turned onto the hilly street that led to his home.

"There are other men who like the feel of women's clothes but still prefer to be with a woman. There are men who feel that they were born into the wrong gender, that they are really women on the inside. And there are men who like to be with men, who also like to dress as women. I haven't spoken to Ishak enough to know how he feels."

Liam's stomach gurgled, and he was embarrassed, but the sound served to lighten the mood in the car. "I forget," Yahya said. "You were not able to eat dinner. We will make sure you and Aidan have food when we get home."

"It's no problem," Liam said. "Our priority is always protecting the client. I want to talk to Ishak when I can to know why he and Havva left the house, and who they think attacked them."

Yahya returned to his own thoughts, and Liam was grateful. It was hard enough to keep an eye on the street, the other drivers, and any other possible threats, without having to get into a conversation that was surely as uncomfortable for the client. It was one of the reasons he and Aidan worked so well together. Aidan could look inside to the clients' behaviors and actions, while Liam focused on the outside world.

For the rest of the drive, Liam thought about how strangely this job was developing. For the first time this evening, he had seen concrete evidence of a threat. But what did it all mean? Where had the brother and sister been? Why had they left the house at all when they'd promised not to?

Was the attack really on Havva, the subject of the threatening letters? If so, then how did her brother get injured? The attack could have been random street violence against two young, wealthy-looking people out well after dark. A bungled purse snatching, perhaps.

Or someone could have realized Ishak was a transvestite, even though he looked convincing in a dress. Turkey prided itself on its secular government, but it was still a Muslim country with many conservatives. Combine prejudice and repression with alcohol and darkness, and you had a volatile mixture.

He thought he had left that kind of danger behind by taking Aidan out of Tunisia. Liam was confident at his ability to pass for straight and had never been threatened because of his sexual orientation. But Aidan was easier to spot, and more open besides, and that put him at risk.

He would never tell Aidan that the move had been for his partner's safety; he said it was because he thought Aidan would be more comfortable, happier, in Europe than in Tunisia.

Yahya pulled up in the driveway and opened the garage door. "There should be food in the kitchen. You may feel free with anything you find. When my wife returns, please tell her that I have gone to bed."

"Certainly," Liam said as he got out of the car. So no mention of his son, or worry about Ishak's condition?

But that was none of his business, he reminded himself. His job was to protect the Farias family from unknown assailants, not from their own internal divisions.

10 – Some Evening

Aidan stood by the emergency room door as Liam and Yahya walked out. Meryem sat next to her son, engaged in intense conversation. The old man across from him moaned in the universal language of pain. The last time he'd been to a hospital emergency room was when his father had begun his short spiral to death.

One night he had been in the bedroom he shared with Blake when the phone rang around ten o'clock. *"Who's calling so late?"* Blake asked as Aidan answered. It was his mother; his father had fallen in the shower and hit his head, and she'd called the paramedics.

Aidan arranged to meet her at the hospital in Trenton, and he'd spent the next few weeks traveling back and forth up I-95, canceling tutoring sessions, and arranging substitutes for his classes. Blake hadn't been happy, but Aidan was an only child, and there was no one else to help his mother.

All emergency rooms looked alike, he thought as he scanned the room. The same hard plastic chairs, smell of disinfectant, weary and frightened people. His stomach grumbled again, and he looked across the room to a vending machine. He walked to it and fished in his pocket for money. But the machine only took coins, and he didn't have any.

Havva joined him. "I can use my card," she said, pointing to a slot. "What would you like?"

"A sandwich and a bottle of water would be great," he said.

She slid her card and punched the buttons. The food slipped to the bottom, and Aidan retrieved it. The two of them turned back to face Meryem and Ishak, who were deep in conversation.

"Why did you leave the house?" Aidan asked Havva as he peeled open the sandwich.

"My brother worked at a restaurant," she said. "He wanted to say good-bye to the people he knew there, but since my parents required us to move back to their home, we have been under constant supervision. Tonight was our opportunity to sneak out."

"Did you make it there?" He took a bite of the sandwich—some kind of chicken salad, he thought. He ate it gratefully.

She nodded. "We had dinner there and then left, to be home before our parents."

Her lower lip quivered, and Aidan put his hand on her shoulder. "What happened?"

"This crazy man, a bum, he came out of nowhere when we walked out of the restaurant. He began to yell at us. How we were evil, terrible people. My brother stepped forward to chase him away, and the man pushed him."

She pulled a tissue from her pocket and dabbed her eyes. "I told Ishak not to wear heels," she said, shaking her head. "He stumbled when the man pushed him, and he fell to the pavement. He reached his arm out to break his fall, and then he cried out in pain. I leaned down to him, and when I looked up, the man had gone."

Aidan gobbled the rest of the sandwich and drank half the bottle of water in one long gulp. "Did you recognize the man?"

Havva shook her head. "It was very dark, so I did not see him well. There have been incidents like this before, people leaving this kind of restaurant or club and thieves attacking them."

"Tell me more about the restaurant," Aidan said, wiping his mouth with the back of his hand. "For gay men? Or transvestites? Or a place where men pick up prostitutes?"

"My brother is not a prostitute! He only worked at the club to be around other people like himself. It is very hard for him."

"Were you close enough to the entrance that this man knew you'd come from there?"

"We were a half block away. He could have seen us come out."

"Did your brother wear dresses to work? And did he, or any of the other hostesses, have trouble?"

"We lived together, so I often helped him with his makeup before he left for work. I know there have been incidents in that area before, but I don't believe Ishak or anyone else he knew was bothered."

He pointed to the Star of David she wore around her neck. "Your parents have both said that things are difficult for Jews here. Did the man say anything about religion?"

"I wasn't listening very carefully. I was looking around for police, or for other people to help us." She concentrated. "Maybe he did say something," she said after a while. "I remember him saying the name David. I thought maybe that was his name, but he could have been referring to my star."

"Did the man call you by name?"

"I don't think so. But why would he know us?"

"Because those letters your father received, they mentioned your name. Maybe this man was waiting for you, not for Ishak."

"But why?" she nearly wailed. "I have done nothing to anyone."

"Did you call the police?"

She shook her head. "I wanted to get my brother here, to the hospital. The police would only have delayed us."

Another incident with no police contact, Aidan thought. Curiouser and curiouser.

Across the room from them, Meryem stood, helping Ishak. "I should find a cab," Havva said.

"I'll do that," Aidan said. "You stay here."

He stepped outside and scanned the area. He walked forward to the street and began waving his arm at anything that looked like a cab. After a couple of minutes, one pulled up, and he directed it behind him to the emergency entrance. By the time he got there, Havva, Ishak, and Meryem had come out.

Meryem settled her son in the front seat, and she, Havva, and Aidan clustered into the back. Ishak gave the cabbie the address, and they were all silent during the ride. When they got to the house, Liam was in the kitchen eating a plate of what looked like leftover *börek*, a spinach pie. "Yahya said to tell you that he's gone up to bed," Liam said.

Meryem nodded. "I will go to him."

"I'll look after Ishak," Havva said, taking her brother's hand. "We will see you in the morning."

The three of them left, and Aidan asked Liam, "Any more of

that?"

"Get a fork, and you can share," Liam said.

Aidan poured glasses of cold water for both of them, got himself a fork, and joined Liam at the table. "Some evening, huh?" he asked.

Liam nodded. "Did Ishak or Havva tell you why they lied to us?"

Aidan explained about the restaurant and Ishak's desire to say good-bye to the people he had worked with.

"And the man who attacked them?"

"Confusing," Aidan said. "Havva said it was difficult to understand him, but she did catch the name David, which could have been his name, the name of the person he thought he was attacking, or could have referred to the Star of David around her neck."

"Nothing to do with Ishak's cross-dressing?"

Aidan shrugged. "She didn't know. Maybe he knew what kind of restaurant it was and waited outside for someone to attack. Or maybe he saw her Star of David and it set him off." He paused. "Or maybe whoever sent the letters to Yahya was going after Havva. The letters did mention her name."

"But the attacker didn't?"

"She didn't think so. But she's pretty shaken up."

They finished eating, and Aidan rinsed their dishes and placed them in the dishwasher. Then he followed Liam to their room in the old part of the house. His feelings were jumbled—missing his parents, his heart aching for the brewing problems between father and son, his need for Liam the one constant in his world.

"This case is very confusing," Liam said as he began to unbutton his dress shirt.

"Let me help you with that," Aidan said, pushing away his partner's fingers. He looked up at Liam and smiled. This was his rock, his safe harbor, this connection he had with the man he loved.

"Aren't you tired?" Liam asked. "We've been on our feet all night."

"Never too tired for this." Aidan undid each button carefully, then slipped Liam's shirt off, revealing his broad chest and the two gold nipple rings. He leaned down and took one nipple in his mouth, licking it, then nibbling. Liam arched his back with pleasure.

Then Aidan turned to his partner's underarms. Liam lifted his arm, and Aidan nosed beneath it, inhaling the scent that was so uniquely Liam. He licked around the edges, and Liam said, "That tickles."

He pulled Aidan's head back to his so they could kiss. He tugged out the tails of Aidan's shirt and slipped his hands along the smooth skin of Aidan's sides, almost the only part of him that wasn't covered in fine, silky hair.

Aidan stepped back and the two of them stripped. When they came back together, Aidan in his boxer shorts and Liam in his jockstrap, both of them were hard.

Aidan rubbed his hand up and down over the jockstrap's pouch as he and Liam kissed. They stood together, rocking gently back and forth, until Aidan dropped to his knees and pulled Liam's dick out the side of the pouch. He began licking it in slow strokes as his own dick ached for release. Liam stood above him like the Colossus of

Rhodes, his broad legs planted apart, one hand ruffling Aidan's hair.

"Baby, if you keep doing that…" Liam said.

Aidan knew just how far he could go. He could feel Liam's body tensing as it prepared for orgasm, the way his balls tightened and his breathing intensified. He backed away from Liam's dick, stood, and dropped his boxers. His stiff dick flapped, but he didn't care—he turned around, leaned over the bed, and presented his ass to his partner.

Liam eased Aidan's ass cheeks apart and pressed his dick against the hairy hole. Aidan took a deep breath and felt Liam's dick move into him.

They had used condoms at first, until they were sure they were disease-free and committed to monogamy. Now it was skin against skin, the feeling of Liam's hardness pressing into him, sliding up his chute like it was born to be there.

Liam gripped Aidan's hips and began to fuck his ass in long, slow thrusts, aiming for his prostate. Aidan's body shivered every time Liam hit that button. Liam reached around and jacked Aidan's dick, his strokes getting faster to match the rhythm of his fucking. Aidan was on the brink of orgasm when Liam slammed deep into his ass, and he felt the hot spurt of come.

That was enough to send him over the edge, his body racked with spasms of pleasure.

"You make me crazy, you know that?" Liam said as he slid out of Aidan's ass, slapping it once.

Aidan's dick was so sensitive the slight breeze in the room hurt, and his ass was dripping with come. "Right back atcha, babe." He went into the bathroom and returned with a warm, wet towel for Liam.

"I don't like being kept in the dark," Liam said, resting back against the pillow and spreading his legs so that Aidan could clean him up. "I don't understand what they really need us for."

"What do you think about accompanying them back to the States?" Aidan asked as he gently cleaned his partner's dick. The more he thought about it, the more he liked the idea. An expense-paid trip back home, the chance to see his family. All good.

"Absolutely not," Liam said.

"Why not? If the client wants the protection, even if it's strange, it's reasonable. Why turn it down, especially when it could benefit both of us?"

"I don't see any benefit." Liam sat up and moved the blanket over him, then crossed his arms over his chest.

"I've been away from my family for two years. It would be nice to see them again, even if just for a few days." Aidan thought of all those family events he'd missed, the big ones and the small ones, and felt a pang of homesickness.

"I don't understand why the two of us together isn't family enough for you."

"Liam. I've told you this over and over. I love you, and you're the center of my life. But I can't turn my back on my family as easily as you can. I have nearly forty years' worth of memories of my aunts and uncles and cousins that matter to me."

"I haven't turned my back on my family. I talk to my mother at least once a month. I send gifts to my sisters and my nieces and nephews."

"And when was the last time you saw any of them, aside from Skyping your mother the other day?"

"Why does that matter?"

"It's a question, Liam. What's the answer?"

Liam blew out a big breath. "Four, five years? Something like that."

"And that doesn't bother you at all?"

"I'm not obsessed with my family like you are. They go their way, and I go mine."

Aidan felt there had to be something more behind Liam's attitude. Why wouldn't he want to see his mother again after so long apart? Aidan had never gotten the sense that Liam's mother had been abusive to him. If anything, she'd been kind, protecting him from his father's wrath.

The wet washcloth was cold and clammy in his hand, and he took it to the bathroom and dropped it in the sink. He washed his hands and went back to the bedroom, where Liam was still talking. "You need to remember that these people, the Fariases—they're not your family. They're our clients, and you need to treat them that way. You've been getting too caught up in their dramas."

"Excuse me?"

"I'm not sure there is any threat to them from the outside. They could be imploding. There's a lot these people aren't talking about, either to us or to each other. Like springing on us that they're moving to the US."

Aidan felt obligated to defend them. "We've stepped into the middle of a complicated situation. It's going to take us a while to figure out all the angles."

"And in the meantime, they could be playing us for their own purposes."

"Get the L out of there," Aidan said, trying to make a joke, but it fell flat. "They're certainly paying us, even if they are playing us in some way."

Liam turned on his side, his back to Aidan. "Go to sleep," he said.

Aidan poked him in the back. They never went to sleep without mutual declarations of love. "Don't you have something else to say?"

"I love you, Aidan," Liam said into his pillow. "No matter how obsessed you get. Now go. To. Sleep."

"I love you, Liam." Aidan slipped into the bed and turned on his side, facing his partner, and pressed one leg against Liam's. Then they slept.

11 — Squeezing

Liam rose early the next morning. His muscles were stiff from all the standing the night before. He pulled on his workout clothes and walked quietly out to the garden, where he focused on yoga, tai chi, and other stretching exercises. He didn't feel anyone watching him, and no one approached him.

Aidan was still in bed when he returned to their room. "Wake up, sleepyhead," Liam said as he pulled off his sweat-soaked T-shirt.

"I can't move," Aidan groaned. "What did you do to me last night?"

"Me?" Liam said indignantly. He shimmied out of his nylon shorts and jockstrap, and his half-hard dick flapped against his thigh. "You're the one who started things."

"But I didn't realize how sore I'd be this morning."

"Sit up," Liam commanded. He sat naked on the bed behind Aidan and began massaging the back of his neck.

"God, that feels good," Aidan said.

Liam was in no mood for a full-on massage; they had a lot to accomplish that day. Using his fingers and his thumbs, he poked and prodded Aidan's neck and back until he felt the tension releasing in his partner's muscles.

He stood. "I'm taking a shower. You'd better get moving."

Liam half expected Aidan to join him in the shower, but he didn't. At least his partner was waiting in the bathroom to shower as soon as Liam stepped out.

Liam dressed and then sat on the bed with the laptop, checking e-mail while he waited for Aidan to get ready. There was a message from Jean-Luc Derain, asking how things were going, and Liam was at a loss as to how to respond. He settled for a quick, *Complicated. More details to follow.* Then he hit Send.

He and Aidan walked back through the narrow hallways of the old house to the modern kitchen in the new one. Meryem was sitting with Teyze Eda when they walked in. The older woman wore a housecoat in a flowered print and soft slippers, while Meryem was already dressed for the day in a skirt and blouse.

"How is Yahya doing?" Aidan asked Meryem as they sat down at the table.

Liam thought it was curious that he asked about her husband rather than her son, but Meryem didn't appear surprised. "He is very unhappy," she said. "But we both agree that whatever else happens, our family must leave Turkey as soon as possible."

Teyze Eda shook her head. "It is not good to have such unhappiness in families."

The maid brought in a platter of bread, fruit, and juice, and Aidan and Liam helped themselves. "I have to agree with you both," Liam said.

They heard Yahya before they saw him. He was arguing loudly in Turkish, and Liam worried that he had confronted Ishak and that whatever had begun to brew the night before was about to spill over.

Sadly, this kind of situation came up often when bodyguards were assigned to protect a family. Secrets that had been hidden or ignored came to light, and sometimes the internal turmoil was worse than any exterior threat.

But when Yahya entered the kitchen, he had his cell phone to his ear. He stalked to the refrigerator and grabbed a carton of orange juice. He stabbed the phone to end the call and then drank the juice from the carton like a teenager.

Liam saw Meryem's unhappy look and was glad she didn't say anything.

"It is these problems with Gezi Park," Yahya said. "They are the spark which has lit a flame of protest."

Liam was surprised Yahya wasn't yelling about finding his son wearing a dress, but maybe these other problems really were bigger in his mind.

"You must understand, there has been much tension with the AKP—the president's party," Meryem said. "Many groups feel that the government does not value them—women, trade unionists, environmentalists, even gay people."

Liam noticed she shot a look at her husband, who said nothing.

"The protests in Gezi Park showed that many people are unhappy and that maybe if we protest enough, we can cause change to happen." She turned to Yahya. "Surely you must agree that we need to change."

"No, the Turks need to change," Yahya said. "We need to leave." He shook his head.

"You will come with us?" Meryem asked Aidan and Liam. "To New Jersey?"

Liam looked at Aidan, who so clearly wanted to go. What the hell, he could go back to Jersey, and his family never needed to know. "If that's what you want."

"Excellent," Meryem said. "That is one thing we do not need to worry about. There are many others, if we are to leave quickly."

Yahya looked up to see Havva in the doorway to the kitchen. "Come, come," he said. "With your brother. We have details to arrange."

Havva and Ishak joined them at the large kitchen table. Ishak wore a button-down shirt and plaid shorts. The white cast was supported by a sling that ran over his shoulder.

"How's your arm?" Aidan asked.

"It itches," Ishak said. "But I am lucky it was not worse."

"That's true," Liam said. He looked around the table at the family. "There's something we need to establish right now, if you want Aidan and me to continue with you. When we say something isn't safe, you need to believe us. And when you promise us not to go out without us, you have to keep that promise."

"But that incident," Yahya said. "It was nothing to do with the rest of us. Just Ishak."

Liam shook his head. "We can't be sure. What if the same person who wrote the threatening letters to you, asking for something that he believes Havva stole from him, decided to follow her and attack her?"

"You think this man wanted to hurt Havva, not Ishak?"

Liam looked at Havva. "Have you thought any more about what

happened?"

"I have," Ishak said. Everyone turned to him. "I spoke to friends who were at the same club. No one bothered any of them, either before we left or after." He looked at his sister. "I'm sorry, *abla*. But I think the man wanted something from you, not from me."

Havva nodded. "I agree. I was awake a long time last night, thinking through what happened. The man spoke to me, and he only pushed Ishak when he tried to protect me."

"You're sure you didn't recognize him?" Aidan asked.

"It was so dark, and the light was behind him. I keep hearing his voice in my head, and I think it might be familiar, but I can't place it."

"I want you to do something for me," Liam said. "Make a list of all the cases that you worked on when you were a lawyer, and anything you remember about them that we could look at. Someone who was convicted of a crime or lost a lawsuit. Anyone you might have met through the office."

"I have already tried," Havva said. She looked near tears.

Aidan reached out and put his hand on her shoulder. "I know you have," he said. "But now we are here to help you, and you need to tell us everything you can remember, even if you don't think it matters."

She nodded.

"Any ex-boyfriends too," Liam said. "Anyone who asked you out, but you turned down. Any girls too, who might be jealous of you. This man, whoever he is, he's not thinking clearly. Maybe he's upset about something his mother or his sister gave you, for example."

Her father grunted something that sounded to Liam like a Turkish curse, and with a start of alarm, Havva turned to him. "That's what he said, the man who attacked us!"

"What?" Liam asked.

Yahya repeated what he'd said, more slowly. "*Bar mina. El Dyo apreta, ama no aoga.* In Ladino, the language of the Sephardic Jews, it means, maybe, 'Oh crap! God squeezes but doesn't choke.' I remember my grandfather used to say it."

The glass Meryem was holding tipped over, spilling orange juice on the white tabletop, but she made no move to clean it up. "I know who else says that," she said. "Uncle Nissim."

12 – Loss of Faith

Liam stared at Meryem. Maybe they had been wrong in looking outside the family for the source of the threats.

"It could not be," Havva said. "Uncle Nissim is very old. This man was not."

"It could be someone he hired," Liam said. He turned to Meryem. "When was the last time you saw him?"

"It must be several years." Meryem realized she had tipped over her glass and began to clean up the mess. "I promised to bring him some family pictures, but then I got busy with other things and I forgot."

"Could those pictures be what you have been asked for?" Aidan asked.

"Pictures!" Yahya said. "Threatening letters just for some old pictures? Even for an old man as foolish and bitter as Nissim, that is ridiculous. Just because this man who stopped you spoke a Ladino curse does not mean it was him. There are many people who know bits of that old language."

"My grandparents on both sides spoke Yiddish," Aidan said. "My father's parents spoke to him in Yiddish, and he answered in the same language, so he could understand and speak. My mother's parents spoke to her in Yiddish, but she answered in English, so she was much less fluent."

"What does that have to do with anything?" Liam asked.

"My parents only spoke to each other in Yiddish when they

didn't want me to understand. So all I know are a few expressions and curses. I'm trying to say that Yahya is right, that there could be lots of people here in Istanbul who are the same way—all they know are bits and pieces of the language. But I think we should look more at your uncle." He turned to Meryem. "Can you write down his full name and address for me?"

Yahya stood. "I have many things to do before we can leave. I will be upstairs."

Meryem opened a small address book and flipped through it. She copied from it and then handed the paper to Aidan. Over his partner's shoulder, Liam saw that she had written *Nissim Makis. Balkapani Sk. No. 62 Tarlabaşi.*

"I thought your cousin lived here in Istanbul?" Aidan asked.

"Oh yes, Tarlabaşi is the neighborhood, on the other side of the Bosporus." She closed her address book. "Like my husband, my children and I have much to do to prepare. You will excuse us?"

As soon as the Fariases were out of earshot, Liam said, "I wish you hadn't gotten them sidetracked on the language issue. I want to know more about this cousin."

"There are a lot of names floating around this case. I'm going to write up a family tree, see where they all fit in. Then I'll look for information online about this cousin."

Aidan had often demonstrated an ability to think outside the box that had been invaluable, so even though Liam thought a family tree wouldn't do much good, he knew a good leader always recognized the strengths of his team members. "Fine. But can I use the laptop? I need to fill in Jean-Luc."

Aidan used a pen and paper to start sketching as Liam began typing a status report. He decided to stick to a chronological approach in his report to Jean-Luc and list each event that had happened to the Fariases in as much detail as he could, looking for a hidden pattern.

He looked up to see Aidan standing. "I'll be right back," his partner said and left the room.

Liam considered what had happened. No one could remember the content of the first letter, but the second one had clearly mentioned Havva. Could the man who attacked Havva and Ishak the night before have been after something Havva had? He'd know more once he had the list of contacts from the girl.

He was writing up the details of the night before when Aidan returned. "Okay, I think I have something."

Liam sat beside Aidan on the bed to see the family tree his partner had drawn. "This is Meryem's family," Aidan said. "I asked her to help me fill in a couple of blanks."

The tree began with a man named Rabbi David Makis. "That's Meryem's grandfather," Aidan said. "He had a lot of children. Evadne, Meryem's mother, was the oldest, and this uncle, Nissim, was the youngest. He's the one who was in a concentration camp."

Aidan sat back. "You know I'm named after my grandfather, right? Because he died before I was born, and Ashkenazi Jews name after the dead. But Sephardic customs are different. They name after the living instead. The boys are named after their grandfathers, the girls after their grandmothers."

Liam had no idea where this was going, but he kept listening.

Aidan pointed back at the family tree. "Havva was named for her grandmother, Meryem's mother, Evadne. The Turkish Havva and the Greek Evadne are both derived from Eve, from the Garden of Eden, and they have the same Hebrew name, Chava."

Liam noted the guttural sound of the "ch" in the Hebrew name, though he couldn't understand why any of it mattered.

Aidan pointed at the other line on the tree, to Nissim. "Nissim named his son David after this man here, Meryem's grandfather, who was Nissim's father and David's grandfather." Aidan took a deep breath. "I know you're going to think this is crazy, but let me talk it through, all right? Yahya got a threatening letter that mentioned Havva. When I was a kid, my great-aunts and great-uncles all called each other by their Yiddish or Hebrew names—my grandmother Rose was Reshke, for example. So it's possible Nissim called his older sister Chava, not Evadne."

"So you think the man who attacked Havva and Ishak last night was this cousin, David? And he was calling Havva by her grandmother's name?"

"I think it's possible. He could have been saying that he was David, and he wanted whatever Meryem's mother stole from his father, her brother."

"So the real 'thief,' if there is one, is not Havva Farias, but her grandmother."

"Exactly," Aidan said.

"Then it seems like the next step should be to ask Meryem what her uncle could want that his sister might have taken from him."

They found Meryem in the living room, looking through the artifacts in her china cabinet. "I hate having to leave all this behind," she said sadly. "But there is no way we can carry it all."

"You could have it shipped later," Aidan said. "Once you get settled."

"We have a question," Liam said. "Based on this family tree Aidan put together. Is there anything you can think of that your mother might have had that belonged instead to her brother? Some family artifact, perhaps?"

Meryem put a finger up to her lips and thought. "My mother and my uncle did not get along," she said finally. "He was angry that she had escaped the camps while he had suffered and the rest of their family had died. Why do you ask?"

Aidan explained about the similarity of the names and reminded her that the man the night before had mentioned the name David. "So maybe this letter writer is your cousin David, and he wants something back for his father."

Meryem pointed at a large framed photograph on the wall. A slim, dark-haired bride stood in the center, holding a bouquet of what looked like gladioli. Her serious-looking groom stood beside her in a dark suit. Around them were arrayed the members of their extended family—dour parents, relatives young and old, and a scattering of children seated on the floor.

"That is the wedding of my parents," Meryem said. "There, in the corner, that little boy is Uncle Nissim. My mother searched after the war and found him in a camp for displaced persons. She arranged to bring him here, to Istanbul. My mother wanted him to go to the yeshiva to study and become a rabbi like their father. But he did not want to. He said that he had no faith in God anymore, after what he had seen."

She sighed. "I believe it was something more, that in the camps they did things to him, to hurt his brain and make him such a difficult person. My father found him work, but without any education, Nissim's life has been very hard. He can only work at very basic jobs, and the woman he married was the same way. Then maybe ten years ago or more, his wife died, and Uncle Nissim became very sad. When I would go to see him, he would hardly speak. And David, he spoke very roughly, the language of the street."

"Which might account for the bad writing in his letters, and the difficulty Havva and Ishak had in understanding him," Aidan said.

Meryem closed the cabinet door. "When I was engaged to Yahya, my mother told me about her own wedding. In the ways of her people back in Greece, she should have become engaged to my father and received seven blessings from her father. Then she should have waited a full year to marry."

"She didn't?"

Meryem shook her head. "My father was from Istanbul, only visiting Ioannina for business when they fell in love. She did not want to let him leave without her. So she broke with her family tradition."

"That must have been difficult," Aidan said.

Liam looked at his partner, who appeared fully engaged with Meryem's story. Liam was more impatient to learn what it was that Meryem's mother might have stolen, but he recognized that Aidan had to take the lead in this conversation.

Meryem toyed with a locket on a chain around her neck. "She told me that when she heard that all the Jews of her town had been taken to the camps, she lost her faith. She assumed that they were all dead, until she heard from a Jewish group about her brother. After she saw him, she felt strong again, but he could not agree with her. That is why they argued so much."

"Is there any artifact your grandmother might have brought with her from Greece, something her brother thinks belongs to him?"

"I have never heard of anything," she said. "But my mother did not like to speak of those times. She tried very hard to fit in with my father's family. She only used her Greek name, which was the fashion then, not her Hebrew one."

Meryem sighed. "My mother would not talk much about Ioannina, or her family. So there is only one way to know. We will go to Nissim and ask him."

13 – A Trip to Asia

Aidan was pleased that Meryem thought there was some merit in his idea, but not happy that she wanted to go see the old man herself. She was determined, no matter how much he and Liam argued with her.

"He lives with his son," Meryem said. "He is frail and does not answer the door himself. So we must wait until David Bey returns home from work."

"This is the same David who may have attacked Havva and Ishak?" Liam asked.

"I am sure it was because he was upset," Meryem said. "In daylight, in his own home, he will be fine."

Aidan could tell from Liam's face and his posture that he disagreed, but Liam had often told him that when a client was determined to do something foolish, the best a bodyguard could do was to be prepared.

Meryem went back to her cabinet. There was no organized lunch, and the maid was nowhere in sight, so Aidan put together a snack of dates and bread for himself and Liam. "What do you think?" he asked Liam as they sat together at the kitchen table.

"I'm still working through it," Liam said, picking up one of the plump dark-brown dates. "I can see how this man, this cousin David, could be behind all the threats. And if that's the case, hopefully we can resolve this quickly. We may not even need to go back to the

States with the clients."

Aidan's heart jumped. He had been looking forward to going home, to seeing his aunt and his cousin and the rest of his family. But of course that was all secondary to finding out who was threatening the Fariases and keeping them safe.

"I'm sensing a but," Aidan said.

"But…this could be a red herring. Or this guy could be a lot more dangerous than we think. So we both have to stay very alert."

Liam stood when he was finished. "I'm going to call Louis. See if he's heard anything new."

"I'll be in the bedroom," Aidan said. "I want to do some research on this place Meryem's mother came from, see what I can find out."

He marveled, yet again, at how much information was available on the Internet. He discovered that Ioannina, an inland city north of Athens and not far from the Turkish border, had been a populous Jewish community in Greece. Most of the Jews there were not Sephardim, though, but Romaniotes, a group he'd never heard of before.

A quick research detour told him they were Jews who had moved from the Holy Land to Greece after the destruction of the Second Temple. They had their own language, Yevanic, a Greek dialect, and their own version of the Torah. After 1492, when the Jews were expelled from Spain, many had moved to Greece, where they settled beside the more Hellenized Romaniotes. Eventually the Sephardic culture came to dominate, and the Romaniotes became only a footnote to Jewish history.

Liam came into the bedroom. "Louis hasn't turned up anything. What about you?"

"I discovered this whole population of Jews I never had heard of," Aidan said. "It's very cool."

"I suppose," Liam said, sitting down on the bed.

Aidan turned to face him. "No, really. I spent ten years in Sunday school, three in Hebrew school, and another year taking advanced classes at the Hebrew high school at the JCC in Trenton. I have a basic familiarity with the Torah and the history of the Jewish people. I've learned about Jewish cultures in India and China, and all kinds of groups around the world who say they're descended from one of the lost tribes. But these people Meryem is descended from, the Romaniotes? Never heard of them."

"You really get into this religious stuff, don't you?" Liam asked, sprawling on the bed.

"Maybe not so much religious as cultural," Aidan said. "Aren't you interested in where your family came from?"

"Not particularly. They were dirt-poor Irish, for the most part. The ones I know about came over during the potato famine. My mom has a family tree a cousin sent her, but I don't think I ever looked at it closely." He yawned. "I'm going to take a nap. Wake me whenever Meryem is ready to go to her uncle's."

By going back and forth between the family tree and the Internet, Aidan discovered that Rabbi David Makis had been the leader of the Romaniote congregation in Ioannina before the Second

World War. Evadne, his oldest daughter, had married Jacobo Levy in 1943 and left Ioannina for Istanbul.

The next year, the Germans had swept through and taken the Jews of Ioannina to the concentration camps, and most had been killed, leaving small pockets to carry on their unique heritage. He was surprised to find there was a Romaniote Jewish congregation in New York City, though it was the only one in the Western Hemisphere. The other pockets of Romaniotes were in Greece and Turkey.

Aidan searched through several databases before discovering Nissim Makis, aged twelve in 1947, who had been transferred from a displaced persons camp to the custody of his sister Chava in Istanbul. It took him a moment to connect the Hebrew transliteration to Evadne, the Greek name of Meryem's mother. Once he did, he felt a thrill run through him—his hunch about the names had been correct.

Growing up, Nissim must have known his older sister by her Hebrew name, since their father was a rabbi. That had probably made it difficult to find her after the war, especially if she was using Evadne by then.

It was unfortunate, from Aidan's point of view, that almost everyone on Meryem's family tree was dead except Nissim and David. He wished he had some more information about the relationship between brother and sister, and what it was that Nissim, or David, felt Evadne had stolen.

Meryem spent most of the afternoon in the kitchen, making some old family specialties to take to her uncle as a peace offering. Havva helped her with dolmas, cooked stuffed vegetables, and *bourekas*, baked pastries made with phyllo dough and filled with minced meat. Aidan tasted one, and it reminded him of a similar dish his Aunt Sophia had made for family parties.

While the bourekas baked, Meryem prepared a sesame-seed-topped pastry filled with pine nuts, meat, and onion, which she called *pestelas*. "These are Uncle Nissim's favorites," she said. Aidan thought if he lived in Istanbul, they'd be one of his favorites too.

By late in the afternoon Meryem had put together several boxes of food for Nissim, and the whole family, including Teyze Eda, had gathered in the kitchen.

"I am ready to go see Uncle Nissim. Who will go with me?" Meryem asked.

"I'll go," Havva said. "I want to see if I recognize David. If he's the one who came after us, I will convince him that we have nothing that belongs to him or his father."

Aidan was impressed at her determination and thought she'd make a good lawyer. She looked at her brother. "Ishak, will you come?"

He shook his head. "I've had enough of them. I'll stay here with *Baba*."

"You must take Aidan Bey or Liam Bey," Yahya said. "Maybe both of them."

"I'll go," Aidan said. He was still fascinated with the Romaniote and thought it would be interesting to talk to someone from the culture.

"I'll stay here with Yahya and Ishak, then," Liam said. Meryem and Havva left the kitchen to get ready, and Liam pulled Aidan into the living room. "Be very careful. You know the drill."

Aidan nodded. He had rehearsed it enough. Check the street before getting out of the car, and the building, or apartment, before allowing the principals to enter. Remain in the background, not disturbing the conversation, but always vigilant against any threats. "I know. And I'll get Havva to give me her phone so I can call here if there are any problems."

Liam nodded. "I've mapped out the address so I'll know how far it is, and how long it should take you. Call me when you get there and again when you're ready to leave."

Aidan agreed, and he met Meryem and Havva in the driveway. Meryem decided to let Havva drive the big SUV. "I prefer my little car," she said. Aidan sat in the backseat as Havva drove down the hill and then circled the narrow streets.

"I feel very bad," Meryem said. "In the past I tried to visit Uncle Nissim each year at the High Holy Days. I would bring him some of the food I learned to make from my mother for the holidays: *rodanches*, a pastry filled with pumpkin, and *keftedes de prasa*, leeks fried into fritters. But this year I was so busy I did not get the chance."

"I have not seen him in many years," Havva said. "I think the last time was when he and his son came to Ishak's bar mitzvah."

"It is sad. Nissim is very old and unwell. I don't believe he even leaves the house anymore."

They got onto the expressway, and Havva said, "We go to the other side of the Bosporus now." Ahead, he saw the tall stanchions of the suspension bridge. He was thrilled to cross from one continent to another so easily, and eager to see what the Asian side of Istanbul was like.

"This bridge was completed when I was a child," Meryem said. "I still remember the festivities."

"How did people cross before there was a bridge?" Aidan asked.

"There were ferry services. They still exist," Meryem said.

He was awestruck as they began to cross, at how long and graceful the bridge was. To be expected, he thought, as the connector between two very different worlds.

Havva negotiated her way through a complicated series of roads, through neighborhoods that were increasingly poor and run-down. Aidan wished Liam had come with them; his partner was physically more impressive, and that might matter in such a place.

Finally she slowed the SUV in a neighborhood of dilapidated two- and three-story buildings crammed together. The street was narrow, and she had to pull halfway onto the sidewalk to allow other cars to pass. The buildings leaned in toward the street, making the area seem even darker.

"This is Tarlabaşi," Havva said as she turned the SUV off. "Many immigrants and Kurds."

"After my mother died, I tried to convince Uncle Nissim to move somewhere better, even offered to buy an apartment for him and David, but he refused," Meryem said.

Aidan got out of the car and looked around. Up high, laundry lines stretched across the street from one building to another, hung with brightly colored sheets, shirts, and pants. The buildings were all of ancient stone, faded and pockmarked, but the doors and window trims were painted in bright blue. A couple of children kicked a soccer ball around up the street.

Aidan thought about the contrast between the large, opulent home where Meryem lived and this impoverished area. He could easily see resentment building from her cousins at the inequitable distribution of wealth.

Using Havva's phone, he called the Farias house and told Liam they had arrived. "What does it look like?" his partner asked.

"Like a poor neighborhood in Tunis," Aidan said. "Not so much dangerous as depressed."

"Be careful anyway."

He hung up and accepted several of the boxes of food from Meryem. He missed the comforting weight of a gun at his waist and Liam by his side, but he felt confident he could handle whatever an old man and his illiterate son could dish out.

Havva took the other boxes from her mother, and Meryem led the way to one of the old stone buildings. Aidan had the sense that many eyes were watching them as they walked up to the arched corridor under the second floor of the building.

Aidan stepped into the gloom and gave his eyes a moment to become accustomed. Then he moved slowly forward until he could see an unlocked wrought-iron gate into the central courtyard.

He peered ahead. A couple of small kids played on the stone floor in one corner, and two women stood nearby. They stopped speaking as Aidan, Havva and Meryem walked into the courtyard. "The staircase is to the right," Havva said and pointed.

He shepherded them up three flights of a curving stone staircase, the gloom increasing. He tried to anticipate any danger, but he felt so out of his element he didn't know what to look for. Though he had spent two years in Tunis, he and Liam had rarely ventured into the poorer neighborhoods; the impoverished couldn't afford bodyguards.

The staircase ended at a narrow hallway on the third floor that smelled of spoiled food. The dirty tile floor was patterned in green and white diamonds, and the plaster walls were stained with ancient watermarks.

Havva rapped on a wooden door. She spoke loudly in Turkish; the only words Aidan could make out were *Nissim Bey*.

They waited for what seemed to Aidan a long time, until the door opened a crack. Havva spoke again, and the door opened wider.

The man was younger than Aidan had expected, perhaps sixty years old. He realized this must be the old man's son. "David," Meryem said, approaching him for a kiss.

He backed away, leaving her to grasp at air. She tried to step forward, but Aidan held her back. He went into the dim apartment first. The plaster molding beneath the ceiling stopped abruptly at one wall, a sign that the room had once been part of a larger one. The walls were a faded mustard yellow, the carpet threadbare, the furnishings old and worn. Across the room he saw an elderly man sunken into a faded armchair.

Meryem and Havva followed him in, and they handed the boxes

to David, who took them reluctantly and left them piled on a rickety kitchen table.

Meryem crossed the room to her uncle, leaning down to kiss his cheek. Aidan couldn't follow the interchange, all in Turkish, but Meryem appeared to be presenting Havva and Aidan. Both of them nodded, though the old man didn't seem to acknowledge them.

David hovered in the background, not saying anything. Aidan stood beside Havva as Nissim and Meryem began to argue. She turned to Aidan and whispered, "He asks my mother for some family thing. I do not know how to say in English, but he thinks we have a *megillat Esther*."

"The megillah?" Aidan asked. "The story of Esther, from Purim?"

"Yes, that must be it. A special scroll, he says, in an ornamented *tik*." She paused, thinking. "The tik is a round case for the Torah, or other scrolls. Special to Sephardic people."

"And the Romaniote," Aidan said. "I read about that online."

At the word *Romaniote*, Nissim looked at Aidan and began speaking to him in Turkish. Aidan looked helplessly at Havva.

"He asks what you know of his people," Havva said.

Aidan repeated the few things he had learned online, and Havva translated. "He says you are the first person who has cared about his heritage since his sister turned her back on her family."

Meryem and Nissim spoke again. Havva whispered to Aidan, "My mother promises to look for this item that her cousin wants, though she says she has never seen it."

There was more conversation in Turkish, some of it heated. Again, Havva translated. "Uncle Nissim says that he wants to return to his hometown in Greece and die there. He insists that he wants to take the scroll back with him."

Meryem leaned down once more to kiss her uncle good-bye, and he put one frail arm up around her shoulder. She turned back to Havva and Aidan. "We will go now."

Meryem led the way out of the apartment and down the stairs. Aidan had to hurry to keep her from going out to the street before he had checked to be sure it was safe.

They got into the car, and after beeping at a couple of children playing in the street with a dog, Havva pulled away from the old building. It wasn't until they were nearly at the bridge back to the European side of Istanbul that Havva said, "I recognized him. That man, David. He is the one who attacked Ishak and me."

14 – Domestic Drama

Liam began to think he'd made the wrong decision in choosing to stay at the house with Yahya and Ishak. The two of them maintained a glacial silence, moving past each other without speaking, until Liam wanted to knock both their heads together to break the tension.

He retreated to the bedroom, desperate for something else to do. There was an e-mail from his sister Jeanne, marked *Urgent!* with a little star next to it. Liam sighed. He was surrounded by overly dramatic people, from his own partner, to the clients, and now his sister.

Reluctantly he opened the message. He remembered something about his sister and a dog. Her old dog had died, and she'd gotten a new one. What was the emergency? Lack of housebreaking?

Billy, you know my ex, Enzo, has been stalking me, right? I'm sure Mom told you. She stayed over at my house last night because I was scared, and this morning she went out to get the paper when it was still dark. Enzo thought she was me, and he tackled her and knocked her down. They think she broke her hip. Billy, you've got to stop him. Please!!!

What the fuck? He had met Enzo Battaglione once when he and Jeanne were still married, the last time Liam had been home. Enzo was a prick, a slimy idiot with slicked-down hair, gym-built muscles, and a collection of stupid tattoos. He was a loser, and Liam thought privately that his sister was looking for a man like their father.

He checked the clock and did some quick calculations. Turkey was seven hours ahead of New Jersey, so if it was five o'clock in the evening in Istanbul, it was what, ten in the morning back home?

He noted with a sense of irony that he'd thought of Jersey as home, the way Aidan had. He grabbed his phone and dialed his sister's number.

"Jeannie? What the fuck is going on?"

"Oh, Billy, I'm so glad you called," his sister said.

"How's Mom?"

"We're at the hospital. They put a pin in her hip this morning, and she's knocked out now."

"But she's all right?"

"Yeah, she's a tough old bird. You know that."

"You call the cops on that bastard Enzo?"

"Yeah. But he insists it was all an accident, that he was trying to talk to her and she slipped and fell. The cop said he couldn't do anything until she woke up and told her side of the story." His sister gulped, and it sounded like she was ready to cry. "Billy, can you come home? Maybe you can talk to Enzo, sort him out and get him to stop stalking me. Please? Mom would love to see you too. It's been years since you were back."

"I'm on a job right now," Liam said. "But it looks like I'll be coming back to the States with the client. I can try to get some time away once we arrive, but probably not until Monday at the earliest."

"That would be great, Billy," she said. "Thank you so much!"

"I'll call you when I know exactly. Tell Mom to hold on for me. And if Enzo comes anywhere near you or her, you call the cops right away."

"I will. I love you, Billy."

"Love you too, Sis," he said, and he hung up.

It was funny, he thought as he sat in the bedroom staring at the wall. His family had never been that demonstrative. Not a lot of kissing and hugging or declarations of love in the McCullough household. But something had changed inside him once he met Aidan. He'd become accustomed to responding in kind anytime Aidan said, *I love you*, and he'd even begun saying it himself whenever he wanted to end a call or walk away. He wasn't the superstitious type, but you never knew in this world what could happen, and he was determined that if anything did, he wanted his last words to Aidan to be those.

Now, when his sister had said she loved him, he'd immediately answered, whereas a few years ago the words would only have embarrassed him. He was turning into a big old softy. Wanting his regular meals, cramping up after standing for too long, and now telling his little sister he loved her. What was he coming to?

He sat there on the bed, not thinking of anything much, until he heard voices raised in the living room, Yahya and Ishak yelling at each other in Turkish. Crap. Back to work.

He walked out to the living room to see Yahya red-faced and yelling at his son, who was yelling right back in his face. "What's going on?" Liam demanded.

"This is family business," Yahya snapped at him. "Not for you."

"I don't care if it's family business or national business," Liam said. "If you can't get along together for the next couple of days, you're going to be in more danger from each other than from anyone outside."

Both father and son erupted at the same time, pleading their cases in English to Liam. He held up his hand, though, and both of them stopped.

He turned to Yahya first. "I don't know what you're arguing about, but I can guess. Your son is gay. So what. He's still alive. A lot of gay men get attacked like he was and don't survive. Be grateful for that."

Then he shifted his attention to Ishak, who tried to cross his arms over his chest in a mimicry of his father, but couldn't because of the cast. "So your father doesn't understand you," Liam said to him. "Boo hoo. My father was a mean drunk who beat me up if he thought I looked at him cross-eyed. Your father has taken care of you all your life, and even now, he's working to get you out of this lousy country and to somewhere you can be safe."

Liam hated to get in the middle of family dramas, and it made him uncomfortable to reveal any part of his personal life or background to a client. He was angry that he'd lost his temper too. Something about this father-son dynamic pushed his buttons, though, and he couldn't help himself.

Neither man responded. "Fine? You're not going to kiss and make up?" Liam asked. "Then at least keep your mouths shut."

Aware he was behaving in the kind of drama-queen way he hated in Aidan, he turned on his heel and stalked back to the old part of the house.

He stripped down and put on his workout clothes. He preferred to exercise barefoot because he liked to feel the connection to the ground as he did his sun salutations, jumping jacks, and so on. He was about to leave for the garden when there was a short rap on the door, and Yahya stepped in.

"You are right to be angry with us," he said. "I have not been completely honest with you."

More drama, Liam thought. He motioned Yahya to the single chair and sat on the edge of the bed.

"When I met my wife, her family was very wealthy," he said. "My father-in-law came from a long line of traders, and he owned several stores in Istanbul."

More family history, Liam thought. Would it ever end? He nodded to show he was paying attention.

"I have a business degree, and at first I managed a store. But then we had the chance to buy the building where the store was located. After that, I began to acquire others, and eventually, when Meryem's father died, we invested her inheritance. But you have seen for yourself the problems growing in Turkey. And you know, it is always the Jews who receive the blame. So one year ago, Meryem and I decided we would move to America. I began to sell my properties and invest the money overseas."

Liam knew the basics, but he also knew that when a client

wanted to talk, it was important to let him.

"Then a man I knew, Ahmet Tikli, approached me to join in a development he had planned for Gezi Park. My share would only be a very small one, but he needed my expertise in retailing. I agreed, with the idea that I would do what I could before we left."

So this was the Gezi Park connection, Liam saw. "And there were problems?"

"Not at first. But then, as you know, the unhappiness of the people with the government spilled over, and the protests began. I wanted to drop out of the project, but Ahmet Bey convinced me to continue."

His voice hiccupped, and Yahya took a moment to collect himself. "On Monday afternoon, I received a package at my office, delivered by a messenger from Ahmet Bey—documents I was to sign and return to him. But there was something else."

Liam leaned forward. "What?"

"When you build, you must first test the soil to make sure it can accept the load of the construction. Ahmet Bey hired a surveyor to perform these tests. It was his report that was added to my package."

Aidan was much better at this kind of conversation, Liam thought. He had the patience to listen to endless discursions, while Liam wanted to get to the point. He stifled his restlessness and motioned Yahya to continue.

"This report, it was very disturbing," Yahya said. "The soil samples contained fragments of human bone."

"The park was a cemetery once?"

Yahya shook his head. "Not an official one. But I believed I knew where those human bones came from. I called Ahmet Bey to talk to him and learned he had left his office for the day. I was very frightened, so I put the document in my safe and went home. Then that night on the television I saw a report that Ahmet Bey had been killed that afternoon—in Gezi Park. The news said his death was connected to the protests, but I know better."

"Slow down," Liam said. "You said you think you know who was buried there?"

"I was very young," he said. "We lived among Jews from many places, including from the island of Cyprus. You know it?"

"I've been there."

"Then you know it is a very troubled place, Greeks and Turks in uneasy balance. In 1974, Turkey invaded and took one thousand prisoners. No official announcement was made of what happened to them. But in my neighborhood, there were stories and rumors."

"They were killed?" Liam asked. "Those prisoners?"

Yahya nodded. "Yes. And the rumor was that they had been buried by the old military barracks. At Gezi Park."

While Liam absorbed the impact of that statement, and the consequences that would occur if the mass grave was discovered, they heard voices from the new part of the house.

"Come, my wife has returned," Yahya said as he stood. "I will tell you the rest of the story with her."

15 – Scrolls

Aidan wasn't surprised at Havva's announcement that her attacker was cousin David, though Meryem was. "You are sure?" she asked.

"Not until we were in the apartment for a while. You know I haven't seen him in many years, and he got old." Aidan noted the arrogance of youth in her voice. "But he's the one."

"So when he said the name David, he was telling you who he was," Aidan said.

Havva nodded. "Now I begin to understand. He kept asking for something, this tik. But I didn't know about it."

"But he broke your brother's arm!" Meryem said.

"I told you, I don't think he meant to," Havva said. "We were trying to get away from him, and Ishak stumbled. It was just an accident."

"You said you don't have this scroll he wants?" Aidan asked Meryem as Havva negotiated back through the narrow streets to the bridge.

"I have never heard of such a thing," Meryem said. "But I have some old papers and knickknacks from my parents. We will look through them when we return home."

The house was strangely silent when they returned. "Yahya?" Meryem called as they walked in.

No answer. No one was in the living room or kitchen. "They did not go out," Havva said. "My mother's car is still here."

Aidan began to worry. Suppose someone had broken into the house while they were gone and slaughtered Yahya, Ishak, and Liam? It was foolish, especially since it looked like David had been behind the threats, and there was no way he could have beaten them across the Bosporus.

"We are here," Yahya called and then entered the living room, with Liam behind him. "I have been providing Liam Bey with some history."

Aidan was eager to tell Liam that Havva had recognized the attacker, but Yahya motioned them to the sofa, clearly having something else on his mind. A moment later, Ishak entered the room, escorting his grandmother on his arm, and they sat together on a divan.

Yahya said something in Turkish to Meryem, and she nodded. Then he turned to Aidan. "I have told Liam Bey about my business. I am sure he will tell you himself later."

Liam said, "The short story is that Yahya believes a thousand Cypriots were murdered in 1974 and buried in a mass grave in Gezi Park."

While Aidan absorbed that information, Yahya continued to speak.

"As I told Liam Bey, we planned to move to the United States, with the help of my aunt and my cousin. After my friend Ahmet Bey was murdered, I told Ellen of my fears. She suggested you could protect us here in Turkey until this situation was resolved."

Aidan nodded. "You felt that because of your friend's death, you might be in danger?"

"Someone wishes to hide the location of this mass grave," he said. "That person killed Ahmet Bey. And may wish to kill me too. It was only after you arrived that Meryem and I decided to leave immediately."

Aidan saw Teyze Eda gasp and clutch her grandson's hand.

"Let's go back for a minute," Liam said. "You saw the report on the news of Ahmet Bey's death. Why do you think whoever this is might want to kill you too?"

"Because they may know that I have the report on the soil," Yahya said. "I went to my office the next morning and announced to my staff that the office was closing. They had been expecting this news, of course, and I had already lost several employees. I offered them pay and sent them all home. Meryem and I waited here at the house, frightened for the next knock on the door. We were very happy when you arrived."

"Anything happen since then?" Liam asked.

Yahya nodded. "Wednesday morning, a man from another office in the building called me. He said that there had been intelligence agents questioning people all afternoon on Tuesday—after I dismissed my staff. Then when he got to work Wednesday, he discovered that his office had been burglarized."

"Only his office?" Aidan asked.

"No. Every one in the building."

"You believe someone was searching for that document you

were sent," Liam said.

"Yes. When I looked at the envelope, I saw that someone at Ahmet Bey's office had not put my name, or my company's name, on it. Just the address of the building. The messenger must have been told to come to me."

"Do you know if Ahmet Bey's office was burglarized as well?" Liam asked.

"It must have been. How else would they know where the package had been sent?"

Aidan considered that. "Whoever is after this document must have a lot of power. From the intelligence service?"

"Yes, the *Milli İstihbarat Teşkilati*—MİT," Yahya said. "They are our secret police." He drew a deep breath. "There is more."

Aidan and Liam leaned forward. Aidan noticed that Meryem rubbed her hands together nervously.

"The building of my office," Yahya said. "It was destroyed last night. The news report says it might have been a gas leak. But there was no gas to the building."

"I think it's clear that you, and by extension your family, are in great danger," Liam said. "How soon can you all leave Istanbul? At least for a while."

"My original plan was not to leave for another month, but the surveyor's report frightened me, and I made reservations on tomorrow night's flight," Yahya said. "It is what my son and I were arguing about when you saw us."

"My father did not tell me all the information," Ishak said. He looked at Havva, and she shook her head. "Or my sister either. Of course, now we will go."

"Until we go to the airport, no one should leave this house," Liam said. "You have a security system, and we will be as safe here as anywhere. Aidan and I will keep watch."

"Eventually the MİT will discover my connection to Ahmet Bey, and the location of my office," Yahya said.

"But they haven't so far, or they would already have been here to question you." Liam stood. "Aidan and I need to put together a plan."

They walked back toward their room, Aidan's head full of all the developments that had come together in such a short time. "Before we go any further, I need to tell you what we discovered this afternoon," he said to Liam.

He explained about the missing heirloom and Havva's belief that it had been David who attacked her and her brother the night before.

"Did he try anything while you were there?" Liam demanded.

Aidan shook his head. "Havva believes it was all an accident, that he didn't mean to hurt them, and Ishak fell wrong." He smiled. "Probably not good at walking in heels."

"That was pretty stupid, taking the client right to the home of the person who attacked them," Liam said. "I never should have let you do that."

"We didn't know David was the attacker," Aidan said. "And Havva didn't say anything to me until we were back in the car."

"I'm going to call Louis," Liam said. "I'll be out in the garden."

After Liam left, Aidan sat on the bed and leaned back against the pillows. He felt overwhelmed by everything they'd learned in the past few hours. Liam would talk to Louis about the larger threat; in the meantime, Aidan could focus on the scroll that Nissim claimed his oldest sister had stolen.

The one time he'd been in a Sephardic synagogue, for someone's bar mitzvah, he'd noticed that the Sephardim kept their Torahs inside cylindrical containers made of wood or metal. He pulled the laptop over and started searching. He discovered that those Torah containers were called "tiks"—the word Nissim had used to describe the megillat Esther that had belonged to his family.

The Romaniotes, like the Sephardim, kept their Torah scrolls inside tiks, which could be simple and plain or ornate and decorative. The scroll of Esther, or megillat Esther, which was read at Purim, wasn't in the Torah. Instead it was found in a section of the Jewish canon called Writings. It told the story of a young woman named Esther, who had been picked by the king to replace his disobedient wife, Vashti. An orphan being brought up by her cousin Mordecai, Esther didn't reveal to the king that she was Jewish until the king's evil vizier, Haman, hatched a plan to kill all the Jews in the kingdom.

Esther heard of this scheme and went to the king, telling him that she was Jewish and that she would have to die if he wiped out her people. Seeing her willingness to sacrifice, the king changed his mind and ordered Haman killed instead.

Aidan pushed aside the laptop when Liam returned. "Louis is going to do some research," Liam said. "See if he can find out who's still around who might have been involved in whatever went down in 1974." He sat on the bed next to Aidan. "There's something else I need to tell you. I may have kind of yelled at the clients while you were gone."

"May have kind of?"

"I did. Yahya and Ishak were bitching at each other, and I got fed up, so I went out there and told them both off."

"You didn't really." Aidan was surprised; usually Liam was so calm and centered, and he almost never raised his voice to a client.

Liam nodded. "I did. I figured Yahya was yelling at Ishak for being gay, and Ishak was arguing back at him. I told Yahya he was lucky his son was alive, and told Ishak he should be happy his father didn't beat him." He took a deep breath. "The way my father used to beat me when he was drunk."

Aidan knew only the basics of Liam's complicated relationship with his father. Bill McCullough was an alcoholic, often verbally abusive to his wife and kids. Aidan knew that Bill had hit Liam when he was a kid, and that Liam had sought refuge in the gym, building his muscles to be able to defend himself.

"What did they say?" Aidan asked.

"I didn't wait around for an answer. I told them to keep their tempers until we could get them somewhere safe, and then I walked out. I was afraid of what else I'd say. Then I was getting ready to work out when Yahya came to find me and started to tell me what happened."

Aidan leaned his head on his partner's shoulder. "That must

have been tough for you. I know how important it is for you to maintain control."

Liam pulled away. "You think that's all I care about? Being in control all the time?"

"Hold on, Liam. That's not what I meant at all." Aidan tried to phrase what he wanted to say. "You're not exactly a sharer, you know. You like to keep things bottled up inside you. So for you to tell a client something about your background, something so personal, well, I figure you had to be pretty upset."

Liam put his arm around Aidan's shoulders and pulled him close again. "You're right. I just feel that what's personal is personal. I know I should be more open with you, and I'm working on that. But yelling at a client? That's not the way I roll."

"I know. You want to talk about why this case is bothering you so much? Is it the relationship between Ishak and Yahya?"

"It's not that. I'm kind of freaked out because my sister's ex knocked down my mother and broke her hip."

"What!" Aidan stood. "What happened? When? Why didn't you tell me?"

"Slow down, cowboy," Liam said. "My sister Jeannie called while you were out. In all the mess of everything else, I didn't get a chance to tell you." He repeated the story. "She wants me to come back home and straighten this guy out."

"What did you say?" Aidan didn't know how Liam would respond. He would rescue kittens from trees, and do whatever he had to for a client. But his family? That was touchy ground.

"I said I was on a job, but that I would get a flight as soon as I could. Guess it's a good thing we agreed to accompany the Fariases."

"I'm sorry about what happened to your mother. How is she doing?"

"I spoke to my sister an hour ago. Mom's resting in the hospital after getting a metal pin in her hip." He stood. "I'm going to wash up before dinner."

Aidan watched him leave. There was so much about his partner he didn't know. Yet after little more than two years, he felt closer to Liam than he'd ever felt to Blake. Was that the nature of relationships—that you never really knew the person you loved? His parents had been married for nearly thirty years, and they had yelled at each other all the time—yet they'd shared a bed every night, his father called his mother "my angel," and he'd been lost without her.

Aidan had sworn when he was young that he wouldn't pick a partner he'd always fight with, and with Blake, he had almost never raised his voice. Blake was an ice prince; he didn't share his feelings, shut down when he got angry. With Liam, Aidan was determined to do things differently. He spoke up when he was irritated, and he pushed Liam to express his feelings too.

His mind wandered back to the story of Esther. In the version he'd learned in Sunday school, Vashti was evil and Esther was good. Now, looking at the Farias family, he wondered if Evadne, Meryem's mother, was an Esther, a good woman who saved her brother after he was interned in the concentration camps. Or a Vashti, who stole her brother's inheritance.

When Liam returned from the bathroom, he wanted to make a couple of phone calls, so Aidan went back to the main house alone. Ishak lounged on a sofa in the living room, while his sister sat on the floor in front of Meryem's china cabinet, with the bottom door of the central section open. Made of a dark wood that looked like mahogany, it had to be at least ten feet long, in three sections. Glass doors protected shelves on the top half, which sat above rows of drawers.

"I am looking for any record of this scroll Uncle Nissim insists we have," Havva said. She handed a sheaf of papers to her mother, who carried them to the coffee table and sat on the sofa.

"Come, I will show you," Meryem said.

Aidan joined her. "All that I have from my mother is in this cabinet," Meryem said. She showed Aidan a picture. "See, this man is my grandfather, Rabbi David Makis."

The photo was of an austere white-haired man wearing a black robe with what looked like a knee-length velvet bib embroidered with Hebrew letters. He held a cane in one hand and had a tall skullcap on his head.

"This is Nissim's father?" Aidan asked.

"Yes. You can see the resemblance there." She pointed at the man's cheekbones, but Aidan didn't see it.

They looked through more pictures and then began going through faded pieces of paper with writing in Turkish and Hebrew. "I can read the Turkish but not the Hebrew," Havva said. "Can you?"

He shook his head. "I can sound out the letters, but I don't know what the words mean. If we have to, we can take it back to the States with us and find someone there who can read it."

"Aha! Here I think is what we are looking for," Meryem said. She held up a photo of the rabbi, a few years younger, with a cylindrical case in his arms.

"It looks too small to be a Torah," Aidan said. "So that could be the megillah Esther."

"Yes, and here is a paper about it," Meryem said. She scanned it. "Oh no."

"What?" Havva asked.

"This is a bill of sale," Meryem said. "My mother sold the scroll."

She sat back against the sofa. "Now I remember a piece of a story my father told me once," she said. "He was a trader. That's why he went to Greece, where he met my mother. But soon after their marriage, his father became ill, and the business suffered. They had many debts and no money to pay them."

She concentrated. "I remember he said my mother had some small thing from her family, but very valuable. They were able to sell it, pay the debt, and rebuild the business."

"Does the paper say who bought it?" Havva asked. "Maybe we can buy it back."

"There is a man's name," Meryem said. "But it was so long ago. I am sure he is dead."

"We can look online," Havva said.

"I'll get my laptop," Aidan said. "I'll look in English; you can look in Turkish."

"If we are taking a flight tomorrow, you will have to look quickly," Meryem said. "I want to have all this resolved before we leave."

Aidan wasn't sure what they could discover, but he was willing to give it a try. He knew Liam would be focused on protecting the family, and would ask for help whenever he needed it. In the meantime he'd have something else to do.

16 – Family Heritage

As soon as Aidan returned to the bedroom to get his laptop, he could see that Liam was upset. "What's the matter?" he asked.

"Nothing."

"Come on, Liam. I can read you like one of those books for little kids, the kind with no words, just pictures. And something's bothering you."

"You say the strangest things," Liam said.

"Don't dance around the point, cowboy. Are you still irritated that Yahya's been keeping secrets?"

Liam turned to him. "Yahya?"

"Yes, Liam. Our client?"

"It's not Yahya, though the situation here is certainly deteriorating. I made a bunch of calls, trying to get more information about my mother and my scumbag ex-brother-in-law, but all I got was voice mail and wrong numbers. It's frustrating."

"I know. But we'll be there soon."

"I have a couple more people to try," Liam said as he sat on the side of the bed. "I'll stay here."

And brood, Aidan wanted to add, but he didn't.

He carried his laptop to the dining room and sat at the table beside Havva. She searched for information on the man who had bought the scroll from Evadne and Jacobo. Aidan took a different tack, looking online for pictures that might match the one they had.

Meryem and Ishak sat on the floor in the living room, continuing to look through the things Meryem had inherited from her family.

As an attorney, Havva had access to legal documents like property records. Most of the older documents had not been digitized, though, and because it was late, the records offices were already closed and would not reopen until Monday.

Aidan had more luck. "Look at this picture," he said, turning his computer screen so Havva could see it. "Does that look like the same scroll?"

He had found the website for a Jerusalem museum, which had photographed many of the objects in its collection and posted them online. "It looks similar," Havva said.

"And the details match," Aidan said. "It's in the Romaniote style, originally from Greece but purchased by a private buyer in Istanbul, then donated to the museum ten years ago as part of a bequest."

"What is that word?" she asked.

"Bequest? A gift after death. So whoever owned it before the museum is dead now. And that makes it almost impossible to get the scroll back."

They called Meryem and Ishak in to show them. Aidan noted that Ishak had replaced the simple white sling around his cast with a bright red scarf.

Meryem shook her head when she saw the image on the screen. "*Ayol*," she said. "This is a bad thing."

"Maybe you can convince Nissim that it's good," Aidan said.

"Look at it this way. If Nissim cares about this scroll, and keeping it safe, he should be glad it's in a museum."

"But he wishes to take it to Greece with him."

"I saw the way he and his son live," Aidan said. "I don't know how much it would cost for them both to move to Greece, but I can't see that they have the money. Could you and Yahya pay them? Call it a payment for the scroll, buy them both tickets to Greece, give them some cash to help them get settled?"

"It is a good idea," Havva said. "If Baba will agree."

"I will speak to your father," Meryem said.

She left the dining room, and Aidan looked at Havva and Ishak. "Have you thought about what you'll do in the United States?" he asked.

"A firm in New York that I did business with has offered me a job," she said. "It's only part-time, as a consultant, while I study American law and take the necessary exams." She looked at her brother. "Ishak and I will live together again."

"And you?" Aidan asked him.

"My degree is in literature," he said. "I was never as practical as my sister."

"My undergraduate degree was in literature too," he said. "But then I got a master's in teaching English as a second language. That's what I did before I met Liam."

"Tell him, Ishak," Havva said.

Ishak hung his head. "I like pretty things. I think maybe I would like to work in a museum."

"New York is a great place for that. There are lots of museums. Maybe you could get an internship somewhere, get your foot in the door."

He explained what an internship was, and for the first time since they'd met, Ishak looked enthusiastic. While they chattered, he thought again about the story of Esther. She had spoken up to her husband in order to try and save her people, even if it might have meant her own death. Evadne, on the other hand, had given up on her people after the Nazis destroyed her home village. The sale of the scroll was symbolic of that rejection.

Or was it? There was no way to know how Evadne had felt about the tik, or its sale. Her husband's business was failing, and she had one asset that could be sold to save it. She might simply have been pragmatic. If she thought her whole family was gone, why keep something that would only remind her of their loss?

In Aidan's family, the women had always been the business leaders, the men the dreamers. His great-grandmother back in Lithuania had run the family's tannery while his great-grandfather sat in shul. His own father had been an engineer and a designer, a man who made things with his hands, while his mother, a secretary and bookkeeper, had managed the household finances and reined in his father's extravagant dreams.

Meryem and Yahya came into the dining room, and Havva explained what they had found. "I wish to go to Uncle Nissim's immediately," Meryem said. "I must resolve this with him before we can leave."

"That's not a good idea. Liam doesn't want any of us to leave the house until we go to the airport. Can't you call your uncle?"

"He has no telephone."

"Then write him a letter, and we'll can mail it tomorrow at the airport."

"We must speak to him ourselves," Meryem said. "This is a problem we have created, and we must make it right."

"Make what right?" Liam asked as he walked into the living room.

Aidan, Meryem, and Yahya all spoke at the same time. No matter what arguments Aidan and Liam put up, the Fariases were determined. Finally Liam gave in. "But only if everyone goes together," he said. "Including Teyze Eda. We have to be able to protect you."

They took a few minutes to get ready. Aidan packed their small duffle bag with anything he thought might be necessary at cousin Nissim's—flashlights, their GPS, phones, even their digital camera and emergency medical kit. He checked his wallet and Liam's to make sure they had their passports and to see how much cash they had.

It was easier for Teyze Eda to get into Meryem's small car, so Meryem drove her, with Aidan, Liam, and the rest of the family in the SUV. Aidan noticed that Ishak had removed the gaudy red scarf from around his cast and that he moved more easily, and that Yahya carried the leather satchel Liam had told him contained all the family's important papers. He assumed that meant their passports and travel documents.

The narrow streets of Istanbul seemed more menacing to Aidan at night. Some neighborhoods had no streetlights, and the only illumination came from store neons, windows, and car headlights. He had the sense that they were going not just across the Bosporus to Asia, but back in time as well.

He saw Liam checking regularly to be sure they were not being followed. Aidan was anxious for other reasons; what would happen when they tried to convince Meryem's uncle Nissim that the tik belonged in Jerusalem, not with him and his son in Greece? They had to get this business finished and return to the house so that everyone could prepare for the flight the next day.

He was relieved when they arrived at Nissim's street, and the two cars parked, one behind the other and both half on the curb. "This is where he lives?" Liam whispered to him as they got out of the SUV.

"It looks better in the daylight," Aidan said.

Liam snorted. He waited until everyone was inside before following Aidan into the house and up the stairs. They went slowly, allowing Teyze Eda to take her time. Aidan could see the strain the steep staircase put on her, and he wasn't surprised that Nissim rarely left his apartment.

David was no more welcoming than he had been earlier. But they all jammed into the small living room, and Havva turned on her laptop and initialized the card that allowed her to access the Internet.

While they waited, Teyze Eda talked with Nissim, and he realized they both spoke Ladino. What a joy it would be for Aunt

Sophia, not only to see her sister again, but to be able to speak in her birth language.

Havva found the museum site and the picture of the tik. She carried the laptop over to where the old man sat. She showed the screen to him and said something in Turkish.

Nissim spoke rapidly in Turkish, looking very animated.

Havva translated. "He says yes, that is the scroll. It is the heritage of his family and his people. The Romaniotes."

Meryem took over, speaking in what sounded to Aidan like a mix of Turkish and Ladino, the occasional Spanish-inflected word jumping out at him. He could only make out a few words, but it seemed like she was trying to convince him that the museum was the best place for the scroll.

Nissim still looked doubtful.

Yahya stepped in and began to speak in slow, careful Turkish.

"My father now offers him money to go to Greece," Havva whispered to Aidan.

Nissim looked at his son. The younger man went over to his father, and they argued in low tones. Aidan couldn't tell who was on which side until finally David stood. His speech was awkward and halting, and Aidan saw all the Fariases staring intently, struggling to understand.

There was silence for a moment; then Yahya said something in Turkish and clapped David on the back. "He says they will accept my father's offer and go to Greece," Havva whispered to Aidan.

17 – Ablaze

Once again, Meryem led the way back home in her small car, the SUV following. As they climbed the hill to the family home, Aidan saw a bright light ahead of them. "Is that a fire?" he whispered to Liam.

Yahya was driving, and Liam leaned forward over his shoulder to see more clearly. As they rounded a curve, they saw the Farias family home lit up as if with spotlights. A fire engine was already on the scene, but both the old house and the new one were consumed by the flames.

"Call your wife," Liam said. "Both cars keep on driving. We'll go to a hotel near the airport."

"But everything we own is there!" Yahya protested.

"And whoever set that fire could be waiting outside to be sure you're all dead," Liam said. "Make the call."

Yahya had a Bluetooth for the car, and they could hear Meryem crying as she answered. Yahya spoke to her. They argued; then he swung around her and took the lead, her little car falling in behind.

The airport was west of the city, and Aidan didn't feel himself starting to relax until they had left the crowded maze of streets behind and gotten on the expressway. He could tell Liam was still checking regularly to be sure they hadn't been followed.

"We should have left as soon as I saw that report," Yahya said as they drove. "I was stupid."

"You had no way of knowing how serious the problem was,"

Aidan said. "And at least your family is all safe. You have everyone's passports and travel documents in your bag, don't you? And you have tickets for tomorrow's flight."

"Which the intelligence service must know," Liam said. "I'm sure they'll be monitoring it."

"What can we do?" Yahya asked. Aidan noted the edge of desperation in his voice.

"We will have a plan," Liam said. "Remember, this is what Aidan and I do for a living. We protect people. And we're going to protect all of you." He turned to Aidan. "Look on your phone for hotels near the airport. We don't want a fancy one. Convenient for tomorrow morning but nothing with a worldwide reservation system."

"I know a place," Ishak said. "It is a small hotel near the Watson's store." He hesitated. "The people there are very…polite."

Aidan assumed that by polite he actually meant discreet. "Sounds good," Liam said.

Ishak gave his father directions off the highway. By the time they pulled into the parking lot, the tension of seeing the house on fire had turned to anguish. Meryem and Teyze Eda were both crying, and Havva rushed to her mother's arms.

"*Pan no tenemos, ravanos komemos,*" Teyze Eda said eventually. "We have no bread, so we'll eat radishes."

Ishak accompanied his father to the hotel entrance. Aidan didn't think the hotel looked that bad, but he imagined it was not the kind of place Yahya and Meryem were accustomed to.

Liam shepherded everyone into the tiny lobby and stood at the door, watching the passing traffic. The hotel, which had seen better days, was surrounded by freight yards and warehouses, and the only vehicles on the road that late were truckers and the occasional small car.

"What will happen to us now?" Havva whispered to Aidan.

"We'll stay here tonight and leave tomorrow," he said.

"But we have nothing." She began to cry again.

"Whatever you've lost can be replaced," Aidan said quietly.

Yahya returned with room keys. Teyze Eda would be on the ground floor, everyone else in double rooms on the floor above.

Meryem took over, and Aidan understood why she carried such a large handbag. She had extra medication for her husband and mother-in-law. Some health bars that would do for the morning. A scarf for her hair, and so on.

Aidan and Liam settled into their room, which had a pair of twin beds with a stained brown blanket on each. "It's a good thing I brought our laptop to Uncle Nissim's," Aidan said as he sat on one bed.

"Let's inventory what we have," Liam said. "Open up the duffle."

He began pulling items out one by one. "Guess you didn't have room for any chargers, but at least you've got your Kindle." He laughed as he held up the device.

"Hey, I didn't realize we weren't going back to the Fariases'. And we can buy chargers at the airport."

"I'm just kidding," Liam said. "You did great bringing as much as you did."

There was a knock on the door, and Liam opened it to Yahya. "You have plans for tomorrow?" Yahya asked.

"Let's work on them together," Liam said. "Come in and sit down."

They reviewed the next day's travel plans. Yahya had booked them all on an American Airlines flight leaving at 1:10 p.m., connecting in London and Chicago.

"Chicago?" Liam asked as Aidan booted up the laptop with Havva's air card.

"It is not close to Newark? But those are the flights that the airline offered. I am not so familiar with placement of US cities."

"It's not close at all," Liam said. "But I don't want us on that flight. We've got to find some other way to get out of Turkey, something we can change to at the last minute."

He and Yahya talked about US geography while Aidan searched for alternative flights the next day. "I can get us seven single seats on a five fifty-five a.m. flight tomorrow morning on KLM," Aidan said. "It stops in Amsterdam and then arrives in Newark at three thirty p.m. Total travel time is sixteen and a half hours."

"I don't want to book them until we arrive at the airport," Liam said. "We have no idea how easy it will be for these guys to get our information."

They agreed to get a few hours' sleep and leave for the airport at four in the morning. Yahya knew a garage where they could leave the cars, to be picked up by his former secretary once they were safe in the US.

Yahya left, and Liam said, "Making these last-minute changes is going to trigger all kinds of alerts with customs and immigration, here and in the US."

"Serious enough to get us in trouble?"

"Certainly serious enough that higher-ups will get called, and word could get back to the MIT very quickly."

He began to pace around the small room. "How are we going to get around that?"

"Can Louis do anything?" Aidan asked. He looked at his watch. "Nice is only an hour behind us, and it's even earlier back in the US. Call him and see what he suggests."

Aidan handed him the cell phone, and Liam said, "I'll be right back."

Aidan watched him walk out of the bedroom. When would Liam ever be able to make a confidential call with him listening in? Sometimes his partner could go overboard with his need for secrecy.

He looked out the window, which faced the parking lot. He could just make out Liam's shape in the shadows, his phone pressed to his ear. He gestured with his free hand, a sure sign that he was agitated. After a couple of minutes he pocketed the phone and walked back toward the room. Aidan stepped back from the window.

"Louis is going to make some calls," Liam said when he walked back into the room. "He can't guarantee anything, but he may be able to defuse any alerts that come up." He shook his head. "I can't believe we were so stupid."

"Stupid how?" Aidan asked. "I think so far we've done a pretty good job. Our clients are all alive despite several attempts on them."

"We should never have let them leave the house. You and I should have been there on guard, and no one would have been able to torch the place."

"That is absolutely not true. What's more likely is that someone might have firebombed the house with all of us inside. You and I would never have been able to rescue the whole family." He looked at his partner. "We can't be perfect, Liam."

"I can be. I have to be, or people die."

Aidan stood and stopped Liam midpace. He put a hand on his partner's flat stomach. "You are not Superman," he said. "You're a human being. So am I. So are our clients, and so is whoever is after them."

"You don't understand." Liam tried to pull away, but Aidan held on to his arm.

"I do. I understand how much you care, and how much pressure you put on yourself. But didn't they teach you back in the SEALs that you can't obsess over the past?"

"Those who forget history are doomed to repeat it," Liam said.

"That means you're supposed to learn from your mistakes, not harp on them," Aidan said. "If you're always looking behind you, you'll never see what's ahead of you."

Aidan felt Liam's body relax a bit. "When did you get so smart?" Liam asked with a half grin.

"Everything I know I learned from you."

Liam wrapped his arm around Aidan and pulled him close. "I've learned a few things from you too." He leaned down and kissed Aidan's neck, and Aidan's body shivered.

"Oh really?" Aidan asked, kissing Liam's jaw. Aidan's dick jumped to attention at its proximity to Liam's body, and when he shifted against his partner, Aidan saw that Liam had the same reaction.

"We really ought to get some sleep," Liam said as Aidan nestled against his chest. "To be ready for tomorrow."

"But we have this tension we need to work out." Aidan reached around behind Liam and slid a hand beneath the waistband of his slacks.

"The tension's around this side, not that one," Liam said. He pulled Aidan's hand back and placed it over his dick. Aidan began to rub his hand up and down the length of Liam's stiff dick. Then he stopped.

"What?" Liam asked.

"We have to wear these clothes tomorrow."

"Then we take them off," Liam said. He unbuttoned his shirt and tossed it aside. He kicked off his shoes, unbuttoned his pants, and dropped them to the floor. He was stepping out of them while Aidan was still unbuttoning his shirt.

"Jesus, you're fast," Aidan said as Liam reached over and unbuckled Aidan's pants.

"Got to be ready to roll on a moment's notice," Liam said. He jerked Aidan's pants and boxers down, and Aidan's dick sprang out.

Liam fell to his knees on the thin carpet and took Aidan in his mouth.

Aidan almost forgot to breathe, so transfixed was he by the sensation of Liam's warm mouth on his cock. Liam had wrapped his thumb and index finger around the base and begun moving up and down as he swirled his tongue around the tip. With his other hand he started stroking Aidan's perineum.

"Oh God, baby, I'm gonna come so fast," Aidan said, pulling back. "Get down on the bed so I can suck you too."

Liam skinned out of his jockstrap, and his dick jumped forward. He lay on the narrow single bed, and then Aidan got down beside him, head to toe so their mouths and dicks were facing each other. It was tight on the bed, and Aidan pulled Liam's ass toward him and held on as he bobbed up and down on his partner's dick.

Liam was sucking him too, both of them hot and horny and eager for release. There was something sordid about the scene to Aidan as well—as if they'd stopped in some no-tell motel for a quickie, something he'd daydreamed about but never indulged in.

But this was no casual fuck; this was the man he loved, the one he had pledged to spend his life with, an Adonis in the flesh who loved him enough to indulge him in anything he wanted. It was the emotion more than the actual physical contact that drove him over the edge, and he spurted down Liam's throat.

Liam was still hard, though, and Aidan focused on him, hoovering his dick like a suction machine, tickling his ass, doing everything he knew Liam loved until his partner tensed beside him and then shot the come so hot and fast that it dribbled out the side of Aidan's mouth and onto the bedspread.

Aidan rolled over onto his back and then fell right off the edge of the bed. Liam erupted in laughter. He scooted over to look down at Aidan. "You all right?"

"The only thing wounded is my pride," Aidan said.

Liam stood. "Where's the bathroom?"

"Down the hall."

"I'll be back," Liam said in his best Terminator voice. When he returned, Aidan went to the bathroom, and when he returned to the room, Liam was asleep, his long legs sprawled half off his narrow bed.

Liam was able to wake whenever he wanted without an alarm. Aidan woke to find his partner standing over him. "Get dressed," Liam said. "We've got to leave in a few minutes. I'm going to make sure everyone else is up and that the cars are all right."

Aidan dressed and repacked the duffle, then went down to the hotel's meager lobby, where Meryem, Yahya, and Teyze Eda waited. By the time Liam had made sure they could leave safely, Ishak and Havva had joined them, both looking bleary and sleep-deprived.

The night was dark and misty, the streetlights haloed in foggy white, the streets busy with trucks and semitrailers. Yahya led them to the airport and parked in the garage. It looked to Aidan like no one was following them.

He went into protective mode once the two cars were parked beside each other, keeping his mind focused and his senses aware of potential dangers. Liam and Yahya left for the terminal, and Aidan remained behind. He helped Teyze Eda into the back of the SUV with Meryem and Havva. Ishak slid into the front seat beside him.

Aidan ran the air-conditioning and the radio to keep everyone comfortable and occupied. He saw Ishak looking thoughtful and asked him, "Are you all right?"

"I am frightened, but excited as well," he said. "And sad! All my beautiful clothes turned to ashes."

"Think of all the shopping you can do in the States," Aidan said drily.

18 – BALL STRETCHER

Liam led Yahya across the lanes of traffic, under the haloed glow of tall crescent-shaped lights. It was cold and damp, and Atatürk Airport was coming to life. Inside the brushed-aluminum airport lobby, travelers moved purposefully toward the gates, past tall cylindrical pillars and brightly colored signs in Turkish and English.

As they waited for the KLM ticket counter to open, he scanned the other travelers carefully, looking for anyone who didn't belong. It was a very mixed crowd—businessmen, families, an old woman in an Indian sari with a gold ring through her nose. Bored-looking police were stationed around the huge, domed lobby.

Yahya went to the ATM machine and withdrew as much cash as he could, Liam standing behind him. Gradually, the airport woke up. Two clerks emerged from the rear of the counter and turned on their computers and the lights above their stations. It was another fifteen minutes before Yahya and Liam reached the front of the line. As Yahya stepped forward, Liam scanned the area.

A portly man in a dark business suit stood across the terminal, conferring with one of the police officers. Was he someone from the intelligence agency? Or a lost soul needing directions?

Liam watched their body language. The police officer nodded, then pointed in the direction of the gates. The businessman took a cell phone from his pocket and made a call as he walked toward the gates.

Yahya's negotiations with the clerk were surprisingly quick; Liam assumed it was because Yahya was willing to pay whatever it cost to get those seven tickets. Liam sent Aidan a text message, telling him to bring the family and meet at the money-changing counter, where Yahya would swap out his remaining Turkish dinars for dollars.

As Yahya was finishing his transaction, Liam spotted Aidan shepherding the family like a flock of ducklings into the terminal. Some tension he hadn't noticed he was holding in his shoulders released. He trusted Aidan—but still worried when they were separated in difficult situations.

Liam looked around for that businessman but couldn't see him, and the police officer he'd been speaking with looked bored again. "We will have to separate at passport control," he said to Yahya. "But we'll meet you right on the other side. You have my phone number, right? Call me if you run into any trouble at all."

Yahya nodded as he distributed the boarding passes, then led his family into the line for Turkish citizens. Aidan and Liam went to the left, under the sign that read OTHER NATIONALITIES.

"How are you holding up?" Liam asked Aidan when they were on their own.

"Good. How about you?"

"I'm fine. Didn't see any threats in the terminal, but that doesn't mean they're not here."

Liam kept his eye on the Fariases for as long as he could, but eventually their line turned, and he lost sight of them. Would Louis's phone calls be enough to get them through without problems? Or would the MİT be alerted, the family detained for questioning?

He hated to lose contact with his clients, especially in a potentially dangerous situation. There were too many variables, too many what-ifs.

"There's nothing you can do now," Aidan said. "Just trust the arrangements you've made. And don't forget the power of money. Yahya has it, and he knows how to use it."

Liam looked at his partner. It was eerie sometimes how Aidan knew exactly what he was thinking. He took a deep breath. "You're right, as usual."

"Can I record that?" Aidan asked.

Liam laughed. They moved through the line, receiving only a cursory look before the bored agent stamped their documents. He and Aidan hurried down the corridor to where they could connect with the Fariases again, and Liam was relieved to see them all approaching.

Under a large, illuminated sign that read *DIŞ HATLAR GIDIŞ*, he found the gate for their flight to Amsterdam, and Aidan and the clients stepped onto a moving sidewalk. Liam strode beside them.

They passed more police, cleaning people, and travelers, but no one seemed to notice them. When they reached the gate, there was still a half hour or more before boarding. He sent Aidan with Havva to get breakfast for everyone and positioned Yahya, Meryem, Ishak, and Teyze Eda with their backs to the wall, then stood beside them with his arms crossed.

"Duty-free was not open yet, but we found a café," Havva said when she and Aidan returned with bags of food and a tray of drinks.

Aidan ate quickly, then took over from Liam on watch.

Liam didn't know how hungry he was until the smell of the food hit his nostrils. He realized that beyond energy bars, they hadn't eaten since the previous afternoon. That was a tactical mistake, he thought. Hunger did things to your brain, caused mistakes and poor decisions.

They finished eating as the gate agent announced boarding for those needing extra time down the Jetway. He helped Teyze Eda stand and then watched as Yahya and Meryem walked her into the Jetway.

He and Aidan waited with Havva and Ishak until the general boarding. As they stood in line with their boarding passes, he saw a couple of police officers walking toward the gate. They were trapped like rats in a maze. Yahya, Meryem, and Teyze Eda were already on the plane, and there was no way to get them off.

He and Aidan could take Havva and Ishak and slip away, but if the police were monitoring departures, they were in big trouble. He felt his pockets. Yahya had the keys to both vehicles, which meant they'd have to find alternate transportation away from the airport.

"What?" Aidan whispered as they stepped forward.

"Police," Liam whispered back and nodded behind him.

Havva and Ishak moved to hand their boarding passes to the agent. This was the moment, Liam thought. Their last chance to get away, if they had to.

"They're going ahead," Aidan whispered, and Liam saw the two police officers continue past their gate.

He focused on his heart rate, willing it to slow down, and smiled as he handed his boarding pass to the agent. The seven of them were scattered throughout the plane, which Liam didn't like, but the most important thing was to get the whole family out of Turkey.

Once they were airborne, Liam went to sleep. It would have been almost impossible for someone, even from the intelligence service, to get a weapon on board, so he could feel comfortable that his charges were safe, at least until they reached Amsterdam.

The time between flights was brief, but long enough to allow Havva, Meryem, and Ishak, accompanied by Aidan, to rampage through the duty-free boutiques buying clothes, food, and toiletries. Liam and Yahya had a porter push Teyze Eda to the next gate, where Yahya managed to change their seat assignments for the flight to Newark so that at least he could sit with his wife and mother, and Aidan and Liam were in the row in front of Havva and Ishak.

"Do you think we are safe now?" Yahya asked Liam in a low voice, while the gate agent printed new boarding passes.

"You won't be safe until that information you have has no power," Liam said. "I assume the only copy of that document was in your house when it burned?"

Yahya nodded.

"I doubt that will matter to the intelligence service. You are still a liability."

"Then what can I do?"

"Just wait," Liam said. The agent handed them the new boarding passes, and Liam stepped away to call Louis Fleck again.

"Where are you now?" Louis asked.

"We got out of Istanbul without a problem, and we're in Amsterdam, on our way to Newark. We arrive at three thirty in the afternoon."

"I'll have someone meet you at customs," he said. "Whoever it is will have a placard with my name on it."

"No secret code?" Liam asked, half joking.

"Of course there will be," Louis said. "What's something that only you and I would know?"

Liam thought for a moment. When Aidan and Louis's partner, Hassan, got together, they gossiped like a pair of teenage girls. Liam had been horrified to learn that the last time they met, they had discussed the possibility of using a ball stretcher as part of sexual play. Liam wasn't so much bothered by the idea as that anything that went on in his bedroom would be the subject of gossip.

"Ball stretcher," he said, and he could tell he had interrupted Louis while drinking something, because his friend coughed.

"I'm going to kill Hassan," Louis said. "Look for an agent with a sign that says Fleck. He'll have the code word *ball stretcher*."

"Will do," Liam said. "Is there any way you can check to see if the Turkish government has put out an alert on the Fariases? Any kind of stop order?"

"I'll look. If I find out anything, I'll text you. Be sure to check for messages as soon as you get on the ground."

Liam ended the call as Aidan, Meryem, and Ishak approached, laden with bags from the duty-free shops. "Did you leave anything in the store?" he asked.

"Just basic toiletries and a change of clothes for everyone," Aidan said. "No need to get snippy." He smiled. "It was kind of fun. Never did such a fast shop before."

During the six-plus-hour flight, everyone in the party, even Teyze Eda, got up to use the restroom, change clothes, and freshen up with the duty-free booty. Liam was less concerned with the shirts and slacks Aidan had bought than with what would happen once they were on the ground.

He and Aidan would have to separate from the Fariases once again to go through US customs. What if Turkish intelligence had alerted the US and asked that Yahya and his family be stopped on entry? He had no doubt that they had the power. And if they did, and Louis found out, perhaps he could do something.

But would the Turks take the risk? If they approached the US government, surely someone would ask why Yahya and his family were on a list to be stopped. That could cause more problems for the Turks. It seemed more logical that whoever was after them would wait until they were settled and then go after them. Or at least he hoped that was the way they would feel.

Yahya and his family had the appropriate visas to enter and stay in the US. And if Louis was able to determine there was validity to Yahya's claim, then once the truth came out, the Fariases would be safe.

By the time they landed in Newark, Liam was refreshed and ready to roll. He had slept a few hours on each flight; he'd eaten and hydrated and used the restroom. While they waited to get off the plane, he checked his phone for messages. There was a single text from Louis: *no alerts*.

A porter pushed Teyze Eda off the plane, and the rest of the family followed down the long corridors. When they reached the lines for immigration, he saw a burly man in a dark suit, in his fifties at least, holding up a sign that read FLECK.

"That's our transport," Liam said to Aidan. "I'll go make contact. You wait here with the family."

He strode across the tiled floor. "I'm Liam McCullough. Friend of Louis Fleck," he said.

"You have something you want to share with me?" the man asked.

Liam lowered his voice. "Ball stretcher," he said, feeling very embarrassed. Why had he ever suggested such a stupid code?

"Louis sends his regards," the man said, shaking Liam's hand. "I'm Agent Serrano. Louis is on a plane now."

"Louis is coming here?"

"If what your client says is true, this is a big deal," Serrano said. "Turkey is a valuable ally of the US in the Middle East. Anything that might destabilize the government is a very serious consideration."

Liam walked Serrano over to where the Fariases waited and introduced him. After a flurry of greetings and thanks, Serrano hailed a porter with a wheelchair for Teyze Eda and then led the Fariases into the non-US-citizens line.

Liam and Aidan hurried through their own line. Fortunately it was fairly quick, and since they had nothing more than their duffle and the results of Aidan's duty-free shopping, they didn't need to wait for any baggage.

When they exited customs and reached the arrivals area, there was no sign of Serrano or the Fariases, but he did see people he recognized from the Amsterdam flight emerging through the doors. "It's probably taking extra time because of the work permits," Aidan said. "Remember when we first moved to Nice?"

"You're right," Liam said. What he didn't add was that there was the chance that something had gone wrong. There were so many options—suspicion by a border agent, a problem with a document, or a communication from Turkey's MİT—something that would send them right back to Istanbul and into the hands of someone who'd already killed to protect the secret Yahya knew. How much could one lone CIA agent do if the MİT had already put out an alert?

19 – Culture Shock

As a SEAL, Liam had mastered the art of waiting. Focus on your breathing, survey your environment, be prepared. Aidan, though, still had work to do on that concept. "Can you please stop pacing?" Liam asked him.

"I'm worried, Liam," Aidan said. "Remember, these aren't just clients to me. They're my family."

"By marriage," Liam said. He tamped down his irritation. Aidan cared about people, because that was the kind of guy he was. It was something Liam loved about him. Usually.

Liam stared at the sliding doors, willing the Farias family to come through them. He didn't need to look at his watch; he had a good sense of time passing. It was nearly fifteen minutes before the doors slid open and the porter appeared, pushing Teyze Eda, who had her purse clamped on her lap. Serrano and the rest of the family followed. They all looked ragged and tired, and Liam couldn't blame them after all they'd been through, from the destruction of their home to the trip halfway around the world.

"Finally!" Aidan said, walking up to them. "Welcome to the United States."

Liam leaned toward Serrano. "Any trouble?" he asked.

"Not a bit. You know government workers come in two categories: slow and slower." He smiled as if he recognized that he'd put himself into that group. "It just took a while to get everything explained." He turned back to the family. "And now, let's get out of here. I've got a stretch limo outside with enough room for everyone."

Agent Serrano led them outside the terminal, where he directed everyone into the waiting car. Liam didn't like having to give up being in charge, but he knew that everybody has a commanding officer sometimes, and the best thing to do is accept your orders.

Serrano sat along the side with Liam and Yahya. Liam tried to explain the situation, but Serrano shut him down. "I'd prefer to hear everything from Mr. Farias right now. You and I can liaise afterward."

Liam could tell Serrano was very familiar with the situation in Turkey; he acknowledged many names Yahya used and asked a hundred questions. He had Yahya go back to his childhood in that Jewish neighborhood, quizzing him about what he had heard, who he had heard it from, how believable the information was.

Liam couldn't help looking around as the driver followed a complicated series of turns out of the airport and onto the highway. Jersey hadn't changed much since the last time he'd been back. Sure, some of the buildings were new, the interchanges redone. But at heart it was still the place where he'd grown up, the place he'd been happy to leave behind to see the world.

He heard Aidan chatting with Meryem, Havva, and Ishak, being the tour guide to a country he hadn't visited in two years. "No, this isn't a very nice part of the state," Aidan said. "But where Ellen lives is much nicer. And you'll have to go into Manhattan soon, and then in the summer you'll want to go down the shore. That's the way we say it here, down the shore."

Teyze Eda sat with her back to the driver, looking pale, with her eyes closed and her head resting against her granddaughter. It had been a long couple of days, Liam thought. But Teyze Eda was a strong old bird, and he was sure with a few days' rest she'd be back to normal. The rest of the family would probably experience culture shock, even though they wore Western clothes, used cell phones and the Internet.

That was, if they were left alone long enough. Agent Serrano had taken over so smoothly that Liam doubted he could interfere if some government agency wanted to take them into custody, or sequester them for questioning. After Yahya finished his explanation, Serrano made a series of phone calls Liam could not overhear.

He looked out the window as they exited the highway in a part of the state he'd never visited, all hills and country roads and acre lots with new-looking mini-mansions surrounded by immature landscaping. Horses stood by a white wooden rail, staring at the passing traffic. Signage was small and unostentatious, and every other development was called "Woods" or "Valley."

Ellen's house was in Basking Ridge, a western suburb of Newark, but miles away from urban grit or commercial congestion. They drove up a long, winding country road and turned in at a gravel driveway to a house set far back from the street, behind a screen of oaks and maples.

Aidan's cousin certainly lived well, he thought as he got out of the limo. The three-story house was on at least an acre of land, with a three-car garage. The front door opened, and a thirty-something woman stepped out. Liam could see the family resemblance to Aidan—same brown hair, smiling eyes, rounded cheekbones.

Behind her was a slightly taller, younger version of Teyze Eda. Her white hair was in an airy bouffant, and she wore a tailored suit and a lot of gold jewelry. The two women hurried toward the limo as Aidan jumped out to open doors. The two sisters hugged and cried, gabbling together in a mix of English and what Liam assumed was Ladino, because of the Spanish inflections, though there could have been some Turkish in there too. It took a few minutes to get everyone out, and Liam looked around.

The property was easily secured, he thought, if it came to that. Serrano was on the phone again as the family hugged and kissed.

"Aidan! You look different," Ellen said. She held her cousin at arm's length. "But in a good way. Very good." She turned to Liam. "You must be Liam. We've heard a lot about you."

"All lies," Liam said, smiling. He reached out to shake her hand, but she enveloped him in a hug, and he leaned down so she could kiss his cheek. Was everyone in Aidan's family as effusive as he was? It was sure different from a McCullough reunion.

He was surprised that she had heard about him—he could hardly remember hearing her name before this whole adventure started.

"Not at all," Ellen said. "If anything, Aidan didn't say enough." She squeezed his left bicep. "These muscles! Now I see what it is, Aidan. You've been working out." She twined one arm in Liam's and

Aidan's in the other. "Come on inside. You guys must be exhausted and starving."

Ellen's husband was at work, her kids at school, Liam discovered. She led them into her dining room, where she had put out a full spread—deli platters, Jewish pastries, a crystal pitcher of water, and the kind of coffeepot he recognized from events sponsored by the altar society at Our Lady of Perpetual Sorrow.

He pulled Aidan away before his partner could sit down. "Listen, now that the clients are safe and Serrano has taken over, I want to go see my mother," he said.

"You want me to come with you?" Aidan asked.

Liam shook his head, then saw the hurt in his partner's face. "This is not about you and me or my family," he said. "Even with Serrano here, one of us should stay with the clients until we know this issue is over, and I know you want to spend time with your cousins."

"How are you going to get there?"

"Rent a car, I guess."

"I'll ask Ellen where the closest place is."

Liam pulled up a map program on his phone. It looked like a pretty simple run, down I-287 to where it hit Route 18, which would take him into his hometown. He walked out to the front yard, where he noticed that the limo was still there. He figured that meant Serrano was hanging around for a while.

He called his sister Jeannie. His mom had been released from the hospital, and she was resting at home. "How's she doing?" he asked.

"You know her. The nurses were glad to get rid of her. Always complaining about some shit. Where are you now?"

"I'm in Basking Ridge," he said.

"Fancy shmancy," she said. "What, you just flew in on your private jet?"

"We flew commercial," Liam said drily. "I'm going to leave here in the next few minutes and come over to the house."

"You'll talk to Enzo?" Jeannie asked.

"Let me talk to Mom first, all right? Get the lay of the land. At some point Enzo and I will certainly have a conversation."

By the time he finished, Aidan had joined him on the front lawn, with a car key in his hand. "There's a car in the garage that Ellen's husband uses to go back and forth to the train station when she can't drop him off," he said. "She says you can use it."

"Thanks, babe," Liam said. He leaned down and kissed Aidan on the mouth. "Be careful while I'm gone."

"Always," Aidan said. He stood in the yard and watched as Liam backed out of the garage, made a three-point turn, and faced the car toward the drive. He waved, and Liam opened the window and waved back. Then he drove up to the street and headed for the highway.

It was weird being back where he had grown up. Though he'd never been to Basking Ridge, it felt like Jersey in a way he couldn't quite identify. Once he got to the highway, he recognized he still knew this area so well, though he had been gone so long, and he felt a sense of nostalgia at the rolling landscape, the familiar town names.

He guessed he was still a Jersey boy at heart, no matter how long he spent away.

He passed the signs for Rutgers, the state university, and remembered how his high school teachers had encouraged him to apply there. He could live at home, he was told. It wouldn't be that expensive.

What they didn't realize was how important it was for young Billy to get out of that house, to start the process that would make him into the adult Liam. It had been a long road—basic training as a Navy recruit, pushing himself to be the best, being accepted into the BUD/S program to become a SEAL. The years he had been part of a team, yet separate, never letting anyone know who he truly was.

It wasn't until he met Aidan that he had fully integrated his life—combining his intellect, his physical strength, and his military savvy with a personal life that was just as meaningful. Coming back here, to these narrow New Brunswick streets, reminded him of how far he had traveled.

He parked half a block down from the row of duplexes where he had grown up, and sat in the car for a moment, preparing. He remembered the way Aidan had challenged him—that he was scared of coming out to his family. No, he wasn't scared. It wasn't anything to do with them. He didn't want his mother crying or saying novenas at church, or his sisters' false sympathies or knowing looks.

Besides, this visit was about his mother and her broken hip, and getting rid of Jeannie's ex. Not about him at all.

20 – What's Been Given Up

After Liam left, Aidan joined the family in the dining room. Ellen had ordered platters of food for everyone, and they all sat down to eat, even the CIA agent who had picked them up at the airport and the limo driver. It reminded Aidan in a strange way of the aftermath of a funeral, everyone gathered together over lox, whitefish, and bagels. Fortunately, no one was dead—though it was up to him and Liam to make sure that stayed the case.

He was glad to get a chance to rest. It had been a long, long day, starting before dawn in Istanbul. "So Aidan," Ellen said when they both had plates of food in front of them. "I never heard the full story. What happened with you and Blake?"

Aidan shrugged. "Our relationship had been running on fumes for years. I thought if I did everything he wanted, didn't make waves, eventually we'd get through whatever was wrong."

"I know so many of my girlfriends who have gone through the same thing," Ellen said. "They pay so much attention to the house and the family, and one day they look up and their husbands have taken up with some twenty-something girl with big boobs."

"I didn't have that problem with Blake," Aidan said. "I still don't know what triggered it, but one day he came home and said he was done, that he wanted me to move out. There wasn't anybody else, he said. Just that he was tired of me."

Ellen snorted. "They all say that."

"I think maybe it was true," Aidan said. "Anyway, I went online looking for teaching jobs in foreign countries, and by the next day I was packed up and on my way to Tunisia." He took a bite of his bagel, smeared with cream cheese and laden with the salty lox he loved. You couldn't get food like that in Tunisia or in France, he thought.

When he finished chewing, he continued. "I got to Tunis and discovered there had been a misunderstanding—the woman who had contacted me didn't have jobs at all. She was just looking to build up her roster of teachers in case a job came up."

"How awful!" Ellen said.

"It worked out all right in the end. I met Liam, and by coincidence I looked like the guy he had been hired to protect—who had been killed before Liam got to him. He needed my help to finish the client's mission, and since I had nothing better to do, I went along."

She looked at him over the green rims of her fashionable glasses. "Really?"

"Well, I did kind of fall for him." He leaned over and whispered, "The first time I saw him, he was showering naked in a courtyard behind his house." He smiled. "And the rest is history."

"You never heard from Blake again?" she asked.

"Actually, I did. He decided he'd made a mistake and came looking for me. Pulled strings, found out where I was, showed up at Liam's house after we'd come back from the desert."

"That's so romantic! Like something out of a book."

Aidan shook his head. "Not really. It was kind of like you'd fire your maid, then notice your house was getting dirty and then go try to hire her back. By then I'd realized how bad things had been with Blake, and how much better things could be with Liam. Blake went back to Philly, I assume, and I haven't heard from him since."

Aunt Sophia asked Ellen something, and she turned to her mother. Aidan looked around the table, glad he had been able to bring the two families together. The only one missing was Liam, who had hurried off to see his mother as soon as possible.

Aidan couldn't blame him for that. He wished he could have seen his own parents—but then, he often wished that, missed the chance to call or Skype to say hello, to ask advice, to share a story.

His mother had died first, of cancer that had begun to grow in some obscure part of her body where it was undetectable, then spread quickly to bones and vital organs. The loss of his wife had left Aidan's father adrift. With no one to prepare his meals, ensure that he took his pills, and argue with him about the smallest things, he'd lost interest in life, and within a year he was dead.

They were both buried in a Jewish cemetery in Trenton. He wondered if he might get a chance to drive down there. He hadn't been to their graves since before he left Philadelphia, though up till then he had managed one visit a year, usually in the ten days between Rosh Hashanah, the Jewish New Year, and Yom Kippur, the Day of Atonement. His parents had done the same for their own parents, and he wished he could be more observant. He tried, when he remembered, to say the Kaddish prayer on the anniversary of their deaths, but sometimes, if he and Liam were on a job, he forgot.

Ellen's sons Daniel and Gil returned from school and fell into an immediate camaraderie with their second cousins, even though the Turks were more than ten years older. Aidan remembered huge family parties when he was a kid, filled with aunts, uncles, first and second cousins, and the way something in their blood kept them connected across time and distance.

With Ellen, Aidan felt as if he'd only just seen her. Yahya and Meryem were a bit distant at first, uncertain of where they would fit in, but by the end of the meal, they were all laughing and sharing stories and Ladino proverbs.

Aunt Sophia and her older sister were even more alike than Aidan had realized, finishing each other's sentences in a mix of English, Ladino, and Turkish. As they ate, they worked out the logistics of getting settled. Teyze Eda was going to Aunt Sophia's, a few miles away. Meryem and Yahya would take the guest room. Daniel and Gil had given up their rooms, one to Aidan and Liam and one to Havva and Ishak, and were going to camp out in the family room with their sleeping bags.

"We don't need much space," Havva said. "We did not bring much with us."

"Why not?" Ellen asked.

Yahya and Meryem explained together about the fire. "Aidan Bey and Liam Bey were so brave and smart," Meryem said. "They would not let us go back in case the secret police were there."

"Secret police?" Aunt Sophia asked.

Teyze Eda started speaking to her in Ladino again, but Agent

Serrano held up his hand. "I'd prefer that we didn't talk about this right now, until we have a better handle on what's going on."

He looked around the table, and Aidan thought the CIA agent could have had a second career as a schoolteacher, because everyone quieted. It was Ellen who broke the silence. "If all you have is what you bought at duty-free, you'll need to buy clothes. We should go to the mall!"

It seemed like the limo driver was still at their disposal, so they crowded in, leaving Yahya and Agent Serrano back at the house. In the backseat Ishak and Havva were speaking in low tones. Teyze Eda and Aunt Sophia had their heads together, and Aidan was sure his aunt was learning everything about what had happened in Istanbul despite Agent Serrano's warning.

He sat with Meryem and Ellen on the middle, back-facing seat. They compared stores and brands as he watched the Jersey landscape slide by. His stomach ached—not from the food, he knew, but from the dislocation of being back somewhere that had once been home, but wasn't anymore.

Could he convince Liam to move back to the States? He knew, from the brief course he'd taken in Georgia two years before, that there were many companies that specialized in personal protection, for everyone from sports figures to wealthy businesspeople to movie stars and their families. And the attitudes toward gay and lesbian people were changing so fast—they could live openly, marry in many states, adopt or otherwise parent children if they wanted. He'd be close to his family again.

But that wasn't what Liam wanted. He was happy to live overseas, to immerse himself in different cultures. He loved the warm weather, the chance to wear his leather vest over his bare chest. He had no interest in being within the same time zone of his family.

Aidan had forgotten how massive suburban malls could be. When the limo driver pulled up at the entrance to Bridgewater Commons, he was stunned. It looked like it would take a full day to visit every store.

Ellen knew exactly where she wanted to go, though. "I'll drop you boys here," she said when they reached Abercrombie & Fitch. "We'll be around the corner—there's a boutique I think Havva and Meryem will love."

When she was gone, Aidan looked at Ishak. "You don't want anything in here, do you?"

He shook his head. "I usually shop with my sister. We wear the same size."

"Come on, we'll find our own way," Aidan said. They found a Gap where Aidan could stock up on essentials, and he was surprised when Ishak met him at the register with an armful of clothes, including T-shirts and boxer shorts.

"I do not always wear dresses," Ishak said when he saw Aidan's surprise. He waved a hand down his willowy figure—he was wearing Levi's and a pink polo shirt. He leaned close. "And the undergarments that Havva wears? Not for me at all!"

Ishak insisted on paying for everything with one of his father's credit cards. "He tells me," he said. "Buy whatever Aidan Bey and

Liam Bey desire. We are always in their debt."

Aidan felt guilty, but he had no idea how long they'd be in the States and didn't want to get stuck doing laundry every day—or running up his own credit card bills for a problem that was a result of a client situation.

"How is your father dealing with—you know. The dresses."

Ishak shrugged. "We don't talk about it. I know he is not happy, but right now he is worried about this man." He looked at Aidan. "You think we are in danger?"

Aidan looked around. They were in the middle of a suburban mall, in the heart of New Jersey. What could go wrong? Then he remembered what a violent country the United States was, all the reports he'd read of shootings in schools, shopping centers, and movie theaters. "We're always in danger," he said to Ishak. "The world is a dangerous place. And yes, right now, your family is in more danger than most. But Liam and I will look after you."

When they met the women at a coffee shop, he was exhausted, and they were all laden down with bags. Meryem had bought a set of luggage, which apparently was full of clothing as well, and somewhere they had commandeered a wheelchair for Teyze Eda, which Havva pushed. The poor woman was almost buried beneath a pile of designer shopping bags.

The limo driver was amused as he loaded up the trunk and then part of the backseat. Aidan and Ishak had to sit with the driver because there was so little room left over, even in the massive stretch.

By the time they got back to Basking Ridge, Ellen's husband,

Barry Blattner, had come home, and Agent Serrano had finished taking Yahya's statement. He and the limo driver left, the kids went into the family room, and Aunt Sophia drove Teyze Eda back to her apartment. Aidan sat in the dining room with Ellen and Barry and Yahya and Meryem.

Barry was a jovial, balding guy who worked in municipal finance, floating bonds for local governments around the country. He was the kind of Jewish husband who deferred to his wife in almost everything, focusing on supporting the family. Aidan had always liked him, though he often missed family events due to business travel.

"Tomorrow we'll go look at rental property," Ellen said to Meryem. "I have a list of houses for sale for you in the area, but you'll need someplace to settle while you wait for a deal to go through."

"You have been very kind," Yahya said. "To open your house like this to all of us."

"It's our pleasure," Barry said. "After all, you're family."

"We're looking forward to having you nearby," Ellen said. Then she turned to Aidan. "How about you? Are you guys going to move back to the States?"

Aidan shook his head. "Not anytime soon. We have a great apartment in Nice. We have jobs that we like, friends."

"You always were the adventurous type," Ellen said. "I would never have had the nerve to go to Turkey and visit Teyze Eda. And then I envied you the chance to travel the world and teach."

She turned to Yahya. "My mother may look very sweet, but she was a tyrant when we were kids. We were programmed from infancy to go to good colleges, get graduate degrees, start careers."

"You had a chance to get away," Aidan said. "Stanford is all the way on the other side of the country." He explained to Yahya and Meryem how far Ellen had gone for college, only to return to the East Coast to get her MBA from Columbia and then begin a career on Wall Street.

"You do not work now?" Yahya asked.

"I consult for a hedge fund part-time," she said. "Just to keep my hand in, between ferrying the boys to after-school sports and Hebrew school and running the house."

Meryem didn't know what a hedge fund was, and Barry, who also worked on Wall Street, began an explanation. Aidan zoned out, looking around him. This was his family, he thought. Over on the wall was a wedding picture of Uncle Harold and Aunt Sophia; his own parents had been their best man and matron of honor. Ellen loved to put together photo collages, and Aidan could see himself, growing from infancy to adulthood, in a series of snapshots.

Was he giving all this up, he wondered, to stay in Europe? He and Liam could certainly get jobs in the States. Liam would be near his mother and sisters, and Aidan could see Ellen's family and his other cousins. He understood more than ever how difficult it had been for Aunt Sophia and her family, and his own grandparents, to give up their homes, their culture, and their language to move to a foreign land.

Yahya and Meryem were about to do the same thing for the

chance to live in the United States. Yet he and Liam had disdained that inheritance to live in Europe. Why? Because it was different? More exotic? Far from home?

He knew why Liam had left New Jersey after trying to live there for a while following his discharge from the SEALs. He was too cosmopolitan to fit in with his family, who rarely ventured far from New Brunswick. He didn't feel connected to the predominant gay culture of the time, focused on Broadway show tunes and artsy professions. He was too much of a military man to be happy at a desk job.

But things were different now. There were openly gay men in every profession, including the military. Aidan and Liam could find jobs in personal protection—especially close to New York, there had to be celebrities who appreciated gay bodyguards, or clients who didn't care about an employee's orientation.

They could make friends, settle down, buy a house of their own…

"Aidan?"

He looked up to see Ellen staring at him. "Are you all right?" she asked.

"Just tired, I guess."

"Of course. You all have traveled so far. When is your partner coming back?"

"I haven't heard from him," Aidan said.

"If he doesn't come back by bedtime, you can text him the alarm code," Barry said.

Aidan looked at his watch. Liam had been gone for a long time, and he began to worry. Suppose something had happened to him? He hadn't driven in the United States for years, and Aidan wasn't sure Liam knew his way around as well as he said. Or what if someone from the Turkish intelligence service had followed them?

"I'm going to give him a call," Aidan said. He stood and walked out to the backyard. Darkness was falling, a crescent moon rising, stars beginning to emerge. He pressed the speed dial for Liam's phone and waited while it rang, then went to voice mail. "It's me," Aidan said. "Hope you and your mom are all right. Call me when you can."

He ended the call and looked up at the sky. The same stars shone over Tunis, where he had met Liam and lived with him, over Nice, where they made their home now, and over Istanbul, where trouble still lurked for the Fariases, and by extension for himself and Liam.

21 – Geriatric Ward

Liam knocked on his mother's door and waited. If she was there alone, how was she going to get downstairs? He hoped Jeannie or Franny was there. Not that he particularly wanted to see his younger sisters, but if they'd left an old woman with a broken hip alone, they'd be hearing from him.

Franny answered the door. She was his youngest sister, the curly blonde baby, always pudgy as a kid. "Billy!" she said, opening her arms for a hug.

She was a pretty, curvaceous adult, the kind of woman Aidan would have called zaftig. He leaned down and hugged her; she was the shortest one in the family, an inch shorter than Doris. "How's Mom?" he asked.

"You know her. Full of piss and vinegar. Come on in. Maybe she'll listen to Sonny Boy and take her medication."

Liam stifled a groan. This was why he lived in Europe, he thought.

Franny's kids, ten-year-old Andrea and eight-year-old Tommy, rushed out from the kitchen and mobbed him, both of them crying, "Uncle Billy!"

He picked up Andrea and twirled her around, kissing her cheeks, and she giggled. Then he looked down at Tommy.

Crap. The kid was the spitting image of himself at that age. Jesus, didn't her husband have any genetic material to contribute to the mix? "How you doing, slugger?" Liam said, putting his fist out for a bump. "Hitting home runs?"

"You betcha!" Tommy said. "I have a game this weekend. Can you come, Uncle Billy?"

"Uncle Billy's here to see Gramma Doris," Franny said. "He doesn't stick around more than a day."

Love you too, Sis, Liam thought as he climbed the narrow stairs to the second floor, following Franny, the kids scrambling behind. Franny pushed open the door to his parents' bedroom and ushered him ahead of her. "The living miracle has arrived," she said.

Liam had forgotten that sarcastic nickname, which his sisters had coined for him when he was in his teens. Back then he had been tall and handsome, good in school, and the star of the baseball team. Doris had been so proud of him she bragged all over town, which Jeannie and Franny had come to resent.

"Hi, Ma." He walked over and kissed her papery cheek. She didn't look good; she hadn't been to a beauty parlor, and her thinning blonde hair was plastered down to her head. She didn't look like she was wearing her usual war paint, as his father had called it, not even lipstick.

"You came to visit your old mother on her deathbed," she said.

"Last time I checked, a broken hip wasn't fatal," he said.

She looked beyond him. "What are you all doing there? This isn't a circus. I need to talk to my son."

Franny spoke to her kids. "Come on. The old bitch has her Sonny Boy now. She doesn't need us anymore."

"You're not leaving, are you?" Liam asked.

"'Course we are," Franny said. "I got a husband to look after, kids to feed and put to bed. You can handle the old witch."

"Neither of my girls were ever any good," Doris grumbled. "And my boy ran away from me as soon as he could."

Liam could handle terrorists, assassins, revolutionaries, and power-hungry commanding officers. Hell, he could even handle Aidan at his most bossy and petulant. But Doris McCullough? The thought of looking after her was scarier than any SEAL operation.

He heard Franny and her kids troop down the stairs and slam the front door behind them. "You have medication you're supposed to take, Ma?" he asked.

"I'm not taking any medication," she said, laying her head back against the pillows. "Jesus will come for me when he's ready."

Or the devil, Liam thought. He should have brought Aidan. He was good with people, even cranky old ones. Liam could have left Aidan to handle the geriatric ward and then gone after that bastard Enzo.

But that wouldn't have been fair to Aidan. True, Aidan was better at emotion than Liam was. But Liam loved him and couldn't torture him by abandoning him to Doris McCullough. She could be worse than waterboarding when she wanted to be.

He convinced her to take her pain pills, which knocked her out, and once she was asleep, he went back downstairs and called Jeannie.

"Yeah?"

"Jeannie, it's…Billy," he said, having to stop for a second to remember who he was back at home.

"Oh, hey, Billy," she said.

"Are you drunk?"

"Just got a little buzz on," she said. "Enzo, honey, pour me some more of that Jack, will you?"

"Enzo's there with you?" Liam demanded. "Where are you? I'm coming over there right now."

"Keep your pants on, Billy," Jeannie said, slurring her words. "Enzo's real sorry he accidentally pushed Mom down. Aren't you, honey?" He didn't say anything, but Jeannie continued, "Come on, that tickles! Listen, Billy, say hi to the old bat for me. Gotta go."

She hung up, and Liam's irritation skyrocketed. What the fuck had she called him home for? To play nursemaid to Doris? He wanted to go right over to wherever she was living and knock her and her asshole ex-husband around. And if his mother had a plug, he'd have disconnected it.

This was no good, he thought. He was a damned professional bodyguard, reduced to a temper tantrum after less than six hours around his family. He needed to center himself.

The McCulloughs had a small backyard behind their narrow house, with a decaying wooden fence separating it from the neighbors. It was overrun with weeds, as always. But it would have to do for exercise. He felt better after working out, particularly out of doors.

He dug around in the downstairs closet and found an ancient pair of shorts from his high school days. He stripped down and stepped into them. He was pleased he could still get them on—though they were awful tight around the crotch and the butt. But what the hell—nobody would be watching him.

He went out the back door barefoot, stubbed his toe on a stone, and swore. But once he began his routine with sun salutations, he started to feel better, more centered. He worked his way through his entire exercise routine, and by the time he was done, it was fully dark, and he was covered with sweat.

He was stretching when he heard a man's voice say, "You must be Billy."

He looked toward where the Damianis had lived when he was a kid. His parents hadn't gotten along with them. Big Bill called them dagos and bitched about the smell of their cooking. They had loud, rowdy parties in their backyard, blasting Frank Sinatra and Dean Martin late on Saturday nights.

The Damianis had only had daughters, though, and the guy who leaned over the fence was too young to be Mr. Damiani.

"Yup," Liam said, standing. "You are?"

"Frank Barrow." The man held out his hand, and Liam walked over to shake it, stubbing his toe once again. "Your mom doesn't do much gardening."

"Yeah, I can see that."

Frank's hand was limp and moist, and he held on to Liam's a beat too long, looking him in the eyes and smiling. "Those are some pretty good-looking pictures of you your Mom has in her living room."

Crap. It was clear the guy was flirting with him, and Liam had never been very good at that. Before he met Aidan, he'd found men for sex in the usual places—bars, men's rooms, and so on, and never made much small talk before getting to the main event.

But he couldn't help it; his dick stiffened, which irritated him. He had a partner, for Christ's sake. A handsome, sexy guy who loved him and who'd be more than willing to provide any sexual service Liam requested.

He was in no mood for flirtation or anything else. But he did want to get a sense of what had been going on at his mother's from an outsider. "You lived here long?" he asked as he pulled his hand away.

"Two years," Frank said. He was in his late forties, broad-shouldered, with a scruffy beard. Liam couldn't see more of him behind the fence, but he had the feeling the guy was portly.

"How's my mom getting along on her own?" he asked. "My sisters come by and check on her?"

"She's a tough old bird. When we had that bad snow in January, I offered to shovel her walk, and she told me she didn't need any help from a fucking faggot. And your sisters aren't exactly debutantes either. When they all get to shouting, you can hear them down the street."

Memories of the shouting matches at the McCullough house when he was a kid should have been enough to wilt his erection, but his dick had a mind of its own.

"You want to come over for a drink or something?" Frank

asked. "You look like you could use one."

"I've got to get back in and check on my mom," Liam said. "You know she broke her hip, right?"

"Yeah. But she can spare you for a few minutes. And I could help you out with that little problem you've got in your shorts."

"Not your problem to fix," he said and hurried back inside, conscious that he was running away from something. It was stupid, he thought, but in the SEALs he had learned that half of avoiding trouble was not putting yourself into risky situations. And he fully believed that old saw about a stiff prick having no conscience.

He went upstairs to the bathroom and pulled off the too-tight shorts. His boner jumped out at him. He stepped into the shower and turned the water on. When he was hit by a cascade of frigid water, he remembered how slow the water heater was in the house.

He pressed himself against the back of the shower, waiting for the water to warm, and began to soap himself up. His mother still used Ivory soap, and he remembered the smell, the way he'd jerked himself off in the shower as a horny teen with no interest in girls and no idea what to do with another boy, if he'd ever had the courage to find one.

He soaped his pecs with one hand, tweaking the gold rings in his nipples. With his other, he lathered his crotch, where his dick was still stiff. He closed his eyes and heard Frank Barrow's voice, saying dirty things to him.

He grabbed his dick and began jerking himself roughly, as if he was punishing himself for attraction to another man. His dick hurt as he pumped his hand up and down, and even though the endorphins raged through his system and he felt his orgasm rising, he hated himself. Then he came, hard, and slumped against the shower wall.

He washed himself off, making sure he hadn't shot any come anywhere, then dried himself with one of his mother's threadbare towels. Back in Nice, he thought, Aidan had found them lush, absorbent Turkish towels that made drying off a pleasure.

With his towel around his waist, he went into his old bedroom and picked up his cell phone to call Aidan and found a missed call. He pressed the speed dial.

"Hey, babe," Aidan answered. "I was worried about you. Everything all right?"

"Everything's crap," Liam said. "My mother's a pain in the ass, Franny's a bitch, and Jeannie's shacking up with her ex again. I can't wait to get the fuck out of here and get back home. I figure I'm going to have to stay here tonight. Franny bailed, and I'm not sure my mom can get up out of bed on her own."

"Do you want me to come over there?" Aidan asked.

"Here? Why would I put you through this?"

"Because we're partners?" Aidan asked. "And because we haven't spent a night apart since I was in Marseille and you were in Tunis?"

Liam remembered being miserable when he and Aidan were apart. "I don't want to give my mom any more stress than she's already got."

"Wimp."

"I told you, Aidan," Liam began.

"Yeah, you told me your personal life is none of your mother's business. And I'm sure she'd be mortified to know that her Sonny Boy likes to get his dick sucked by another man."

"You're an asshole, you know that?"

"That never bothered you when you wanted to stick your dick there."

"You stay there with your happy little family," Liam said. "I'll find a nurse to hire in the morning, and then I'll come get you and we'll head for home."

He hung up before Aidan could complain.

22 – FAMILY AND STRANGERS

Aidan awoke the next morning to the sound of Ellen's doorbell, which played a classical march. He looked at the narrow bed next to his—empty and unused. So Liam had stayed at his mother's the night before.

He heard Ellen's voice float up the stairs. "Aidan? You up? You've got company."

He scrambled into a pair of shorts and a T-shirt and went down the stairs barefoot. He was surprised when he got to the bottom to see Louis Fleck.

Louis was about forty, a bear of a guy with a bulky build who was even hairier than Aidan. His head was shaved, but he had a dark mustache and goatee. He looked rumpled, as if he had just gotten off a plane.

"Louis? What are you doing here?"

"Didn't Liam tell you I was coming?"

"No." He looked behind him to see Ellen standing in the doorway of the kitchen. "You want something to eat?"

"I'd kill for a cup of coffee," Louis said.

"No need for that," Aidan said, though he was curious if Louis was armed. Usually when he and Liam went out with Louis and Hassan, the tails of Louis's casual shirt hung over his waist, concealing a handgun on his belt. Today, his shirt was neatly tucked, though he did have a backpack slung over one shoulder, and Aidan assumed federal agents could carry weapons on a plane with the proper ID.

He introduced Louis to Ellen. Barry had already gone to work, the boys to school, and the Fariases were all still asleep.

"Where's Liam?" Louis asked as Ellen poured coffee for them at the kitchen table.

"At his mother's."

"Ouch," Louis said, and Aidan wondered how much of Liam's personal life Louis knew about. According to Liam, he'd never known that the undercover CIA agent was gay until Aidan figured it out, and until then he and Louis had only been business acquaintances. Aidan remembered a comment Liam had repeated to him during the winter, that he thought maybe Louis and Hassan both had crushes on Liam. Aidan had been momentarily jealous, but confident his partner would never stray.

Ellen left them to talk and went upstairs. Louis had been flown in from France to take charge, he said. The Agency wanted to know what Yahya knew, to judge his reliability and that of Liam and Aidan. "Since I know you both, and I brought in the first tip, they put me on the job."

He sipped his coffee. "You've seen this report that Farias claims was sent to him, the one that said there were bone fragments in a soil sample taken at the park?"

Aidan shook his head. "Yahya told us about it. But it was in the safe at his house, which means it was probably destroyed in the fire."

"So you have no real proof?"

"Other than the death of the lead developer, the bombing at

Yahya's office, and the fire at his house," Aidan said.

"You can add the death of the surveyor to that list," Louis said.

"You know that?"

Louis nodded. "Did some research, turned up his 'accidental' death a couple of days after he filed the report, which has disappeared from any official archives. So everything we have right now is circumstantial. Yahya's word against the Turkish government."

"But can't you do your own tests? Take soil samples from the site like the surveyor did and then get them tested."

"That kind of evidence wouldn't hold up," Louis said. "The Turkish government would insist that we'd fabricated the results."

Aidan picked up his mug. "So if Yahya doesn't have the proof anymore, and there's no way to get it again, then what are you doing here?"

"I asked that question myself," Louis said. "But I work for the government. When I receive orders to travel, I get on a plane."

"Come on, Louis. You must have some idea, some plan."

Louis looked down at his coffee cup, and Aidan felt a zing of triumph. Yup, Louis had something up his sleeve, which he didn't want to reveal to Aidan, who was only Liam's plus-one, after all, not a military vet like Liam.

"I kind of do," Louis said, looking up. "I was hoping to get down to Baltimore."

Aidan's brain ran through a dozen reasons why Louis could need to get to Maryland. Was there a Turkish expat community there?

Some known terrorism cell that might be connected?

Then Louis said, "To see my parents. I haven't been stateside in years, and they've been bugging me."

"Your parents?"

"Yeah, you know, the whole birds-and-bees thing? The sperm and the ovum and all that?"

"I think I heard about that when I was a kid," Aidan said drily. "So that's it? Just a personal jaunt at government expense?"

"If that was my only reason, I'd have gone directly there," Louis said. "Instead of busting my ass to come out here and check on you and Liam."

Aidan felt abashed. But then he remembered that Louis was a trained intelligence agent, and there probably was a real reason for him to be there, one he wasn't ready to share with Aidan yet.

Ellen returned to the kitchen with Meryem and Yahya, and they were all introduced. "Agent Serrano briefed me about your conversation yesterday," Louis said. "But if you don't mind, I'd like to speak to you both to clarify points."

Meryem remained in the kitchen to prepare breakfast for her family. Louis and Yahya went into Barry's den to talk, and Ellen and Aidan ended up in the living room.

"You look really buff, cuz," she said. "More, I don't know, mature. Adult. This new life agrees with you."

Aidan hadn't considered how he'd look to Ellen and her family; after all, he'd only been away a couple of years. But during that time, he'd begun to work out regularly with Liam, and he'd tested his skills in a number of different situations. "Time catches up to all of us," he said. "But yeah, my life agrees with me."

"I'm glad you got rid of that stick Blake," she said. "I'll tell you, on Wall Street you run into a lot of dull characters, but he took boring to a new level."

"He wasn't that bad," Aidan protested, irritated at having to defend the man who had kicked him to the curb after eleven years. "He wasn't comfortable around strangers."

"Family shouldn't be strangers. I only got to meet Liam for a few minutes yesterday, but I can already tell he's a much better match for you." She curled a leg under her and said, "So, tell me about your life, more than I've gotten from Facebook posts. Have you protected anybody famous?"

"Nobody you'd have heard of," Aidan said. "Mostly it's boring stuff, waiting around outside hotel rooms and meeting rooms. We have had some adventures, though." He entertained her until Havva and Ishak came downstairs, Ishak still favoring the arm in the cast, and Louis traded their father for their mother. Then Aunt Sophia and Teyze Eda came by, and the house was full of the buzz of family.

Louis found Aidan when he'd finished speaking with each of the Fariases. "I spoke to Liam," he said. "He's stuck at his mother's, trying to find an aide to stay with her. He said he'd come back here when he finished, but I don't want to wait."

"Let me guess, he told you not to go over there," Aidan said.

"Right in one. But I'm kind of curious to meet his mother. Aren't you?"

"You have the address?"

"I work for the federal government," Louis said. "Of course I do."

Aidan had grown up in the suburbs of Trenton, to the south of where they were, but his father's family was from Newark, and he'd spent a lot of his childhood in the car, going from grandparents to aunts and uncles. He'd also gone to more than a dozen family funerals by the time he was ten, but that was another story. He had a basic familiarity with North Jersey roads, and between that and the map app on his phone, he navigated for Louis as they drove.

When they approached Liam's family home, they had to move the last block slowly because they were following an ice cream truck playing a tinny rendition of Handel's *Messiah*.

"*Onward brothers, march still onward,*" Louis said as he parked on the street.

"Side by side and hand in hand," Aidan said.

"Maybe not in this neighborhood," Louis said.

As they walked up the sidewalk, a Jamaican woman strode out of a house with a run-down porch. "I wouldn't work for that lady if she was the last one on earth," she said as they passed her.

"Sounds like Liam is having a good morning," Louis said.

The woman had left the front door open, and Louis rapped on the jamb and walked in. "Liam? You here?"

An elderly blonde woman in a ratty housecoat sat reclined in a chair in the living room. "Who the fuck are you?" she demanded.

"You must be Mrs. McCullough," Louis said, walking over to

her. "Your son described you very well."

Aidan stood by the door, taking it all in. He'd heard bits and pieces of Liam's childhood, but it was another thing entirely to see the house where he'd grown up. Liam had no photos of his family; the first time Aidan had seen Doris's face was when he walked past the computer as Liam was Skyping with her.

That woman had been beautiful, with a lacquered blonde bouffant and perfect makeup. The woman in the chair couldn't be the same one, with her mouth curdled, clutching a half-smoked cigarette in her hand. The house smelled of tobacco and mold, and it was clear Doris hadn't done anything to take care of it for years. There was a water stain down one wall, and the carpet was worn and frayed.

Was this how Liam had grown up? Aidan's heart broke to think of that cute little boy in his baseball uniform, the one in the big photo on the mantel, growing up in such a sad, impoverished place.

But perhaps that was his middle-class prejudice, he thought as Louis leaned over the woman who had to be Doris McCullough and spoke to her. Just because he'd grown up in an upper-middle-class home in the suburbs didn't mean Liam's childhood had been a bad one because his family was poor.

"I told you not to come here," Liam said. He stood in the doorway that led to the kitchen, wearing a New Brunswick High T-shirt that read *Zebra Baseball*. It was way too small to cover his impressive chest, meaning the fabric clung to his pecs like a second skin and the hemline rode two inches above Liam's narrow waist.

The gym shorts he wore were tight, showing a clear outline of his partner's three-piece set.

"Nice to see you too, Liam," Louis said, reaching out to shake his hand.

"Who the fuck is this Liam you keep talking about?" Doris said.

"I wasn't going to stay Little Billy all my life, Ma," Liam said. "And I sure as hell wasn't going to take on my asshole father's name."

"Liam sounds like a fairy name," she said. "And you show some respect for your father. He gave you life, remember."

"Yeah, I remember he used to say he gave me life, and he could take it away just as easily," Liam said. "Oh, and that when he was mad at any of us, he said he should have shot his wad down the toilet instead of into you. So cut the crap."

Aidan felt like he'd stepped into the middle of a terrible reality show. He was sorry he'd ever wanted to meet Liam's mother or see where Liam had grown up. He just wanted to get out.

"Who are you?" Doris said to him. "Another one of the bodyguards Billy works with? Though you look half a fairy yourself."

"Not just half, sweetheart," Aidan said in a syrupy voice. He walked right over to her, leaned down, and kissed her cheek. "I'm one hundred percent homosexual. And I suck your Sonny Boy's dick on a regular basis."

"Aidan!" Liam said.

Doris looked from Aidan to her son. "It was the military that did it, wasn't it?" she asked him. "Made you queer? I knew there was something strange about you wanting to stay in the service for so long, all those men around you."

Aidan couldn't read the look on his partner's face. Was he angry? Sad? About to explode?

"I've been gay since I was born, Ma," Liam finally said. "You didn't make me that way. The military didn't either. God did."

The front door swung open, and Aidan turned to see who was there. A younger version of Doris McCullough, tall and blonde and almost movie-star beautiful, accompanied by a short, dark-haired guy who screamed Mafia connections. "Enzo came to apologize, Ma," the woman said.

23 – Fear and Longing

Liam didn't know who he wanted to hit first. Louis, who'd come to the house though Liam had expressly told him not to. Aidan, who'd just outed him to his mother. Doris herself, who deserved every bit of hell that was awaiting her. Jeannie, who had been a dumb slut since she hit puberty. Or the asshole Enzo, who'd kicked this whole drama off by knocking down his mother.

"Don't be mad, Billy," Jeannie said. "Enzo's real sorry. Aren't you, Enzo?"

"Yeah, Mrs. M," he said. "You know I didn't mean to knock you over, right? I was just looking for Jeannie." He grabbed her around the waist and pulled her close to him. "I get kind of crazy without my Jeannie Beannie to look after me."

Instead of confronting anyone, though, Liam saw his escape route. "Gotta do some work, Ma," he said, and he strode across the living room toward the front door, hoping whoever had the keys to the car that had brought Aidan and Louis to New Brunswick would follow.

As he passed Enzo, he flicked the shorter man under the chin. "Push her again, douche bag, and you'll see what it feels like to break a few bones."

Enzo bristled, but by the time he could say anything, Liam was already out the door.

Fortunately, Aidan and Louis were right behind him. "Where's the car?" Liam asked.

"The red Toyota," Louis said. "You don't want shoes or anything?"

"I just want to get away from here as soon as possible."

Louis beeped the car open, and Liam opened the back door. "After you, cocksucker," he said, shoving Aidan forward.

"Liam…" Aidan began, but Liam pushed him roughly into the car and then followed him in as Louis got into the driver's seat.

"Drive," Liam said. "Anywhere. Just get the hell out of here."

Louis put the car in gear and pulled away from the curb. Liam reached over and grabbed Aidan's balls and twisted, and his partner yelped. Liam silenced him by putting his mouth on Aidan's, kissing him hard. He had an animal urge to dominate this man, to punish him for what he'd said, but also to thank him, in a strange way, for forcing the issue, because after all, they loved each other.

"Hey, keep your clothes on back there," Louis said.

Liam broke the kiss for a moment. "I'll deal with you later," he said. "Just shut up and drive."

He pushed Aidan down on the backseat and climbed on top of him, then ground his hard dick against his partner's belly. The fabric of his gym shorts was so old and worn that the seam split at the ass, but he didn't care as he humped up and down, caught in passion.

He heard Aidan panting beneath him and realized he had an arm blocking his partner's windpipe. He looked down to see Aidan's eyes wide with fear and lust, and that drove Liam over the edge. He howled, a combination of pleasure and pain, then pulled back from

Aidan. He saw his partner was still hard, so he reached over and rubbed Aidan's dick roughly, until Aidan gasped and his body shivered with orgasm.

"Jesus, you two," Louis said. "It's like an X-rated movie back there. Can't you guys wait to get it on in private?"

"You'll have a story to tell Hassan when you get home," Liam said. He felt like some kind of wild animal, a lion on the Serengeti who had devoured his prey and was now licking his chops contentedly in the sunshine.

As Aidan sat up, Liam settled back against the seat and waved his finger at Louis. "Find us a clothing store, will you?"

"At your service," Louis grumbled.

Liam looked down. A wet spot stained Aidan's khakis, and he could feel that his ass hung out of his shorts. But he was happier than he'd been in quite a while.

The streets and landmarks rushed past. Liquor stores, karate dojos, dry cleaners, and strip bars. Same old Jersey. After consulting his GPS a couple of times, Louis pulled up at a thrift store. "You'll have to do the shopping," Liam said. "Neither of us can go in there."

"The shit that I do to serve my country," Louis said, slamming the gearshift into park. "You're what, a forty-two waist?"

Liam knew Louis was fucking with him. "Thirty-eight, asshole," he said. "Both of us. Now skedaddle. I've got some business to discuss with my partner."

"No business that can get any of us arrested," Louis said as he climbed out of the car.

Liam turned to his partner. Aidan had moved back against the car door, putting as much space between him and Liam as he could.

"Are you scared of me?" Liam asked, his arms crossed over his chest. "Because you should be."

Aidan sat up straight. "I'm not the one who was too chickenshit to come out to his mother."

"That's absolutely true." Liam relaxed his posture, then leaned over and kissed Aidan gently on the lips. "And I appreciate that you can be strong when I'm not."

Aidan slumped against the door and faced him. "You're not pissed?"

"Of course I am. We've had this conversation a hundred times. It should be each gay man's choice as to when and how he comes out. You took that choice away from me." He held up his hand. "You were right to do it, though. Otherwise I'd never have said anything, and I'd have gone back to Europe to hide."

He surprised himself with his reaction. He was actually glad Aidan had pushed the issue. It was on the table, and that was that. Move on.

"So why did you guys come looking for me?"

"We both wanted to meet your mother," Aidan said.

Liam laughed. "Well, you got to do that. Now you see why I don't have much to do with my family. But seriously. Who's watching the clients?"

"I didn't think they needed watching anymore," Aidan said. "We're safe in the US, right?"

"Why do you think Louis is here? Because everything is hunky-dory?"

"He wouldn't tell me."

Louis came out the front door with a big shopping bag. "I hope you don't mind wearing a used jockstrap," he said as he tossed the bag into the front seat and then slid in beside it. "I checked to make sure it didn't have come or piss stains."

"You're a prince," Liam said. "We need to get back to Basking Ridge ASAP. My partner here appears to have left our clients unguarded."

"Don't worry about them," Louis said. "I called Serrano. He's babysitting."

Liam looked at Aidan, who shrugged. "So, Louis, you want to tell us what you're doing here?" Liam asked.

"Right now, I'm going to find a gas station with a men's room where you guys can change," Louis said. "Then we'll talk."

Louis followed the GPS to Route 1 and found a busy, clean-looking station a few blocks down. "One at a time," he said to them as he pulled in. "No funny business."

Aidan grabbed the shopping bag, and holding it in front of him, he walked toward the restroom. A steady stream of cars, trucks, and delivery vans came and went as Liam leaned onto the front seat. "So," he said to Louis. "What's up?"

"I don't want to have to say it twice." Louis shifted around to look at Liam. "Zebras?"

Liam was confused for a moment until he realized the emblem

on his shirt. "Our school mascot," he said.

"Let me guess. Lots of division between black and white students? Or your teams were so bad they were like prey on the savanna?"

"I have no idea where the name came from," Liam said. "Though I admit, it was embarrassing sometimes when we played Lions or Tigers."

"Or Bears, oh my," Louis said.

Liam laughed. It was good to have friends, he thought. He'd been without them for way too long.

Aidan stepped out of the restroom wearing the same pair of khakis he'd worn in. Liam got out of the car and walked toward him, fully aware that his ass was exposed to the air and not really caring.

"You can have your pick of what's there," Aidan said as he handed him the bag. "I just cleaned up and used the hand dryer."

Liam took the bag and stalked into the restroom. Both pants were the right waist size, though one was longer than the other. But Louis had been deliberately wicked; both were in colors that should have been reserved for sherbet—bright orange or lime green. The green ones were longer, though the waist was looser, and Louis hadn't bought a belt.

He held the jockstrap up to his nose and sniffed. It smelled clean enough. It was kind of freaky that Louis knew he wore a jock and Aidan boxers, but he figured Aidan and Hassan had gossiped often enough about underwear.

The shirt was a white polo, with a blue rampant lion on the

breast. He had a sudden memory of shopping as a kid, his mom always worried about how much things cost. He hadn't cared about clothes then, and still didn't, though he wasn't thrilled about wearing bright green pants. His sisters had cared, constantly lobbying for designer clothes because their friends had them, or because they'd seen an ad on TV.

It hadn't been easy to be Doris McCullough, he thought. She'd made a mistake in picking Big Bill, when apparently she'd had a lot of suitors, being as pretty as she was. Big Bill had drunk most of his paycheck, leaving Doris to work on a factory line at the Revlon plant, where at least she could buy her cosmetics at an employee discount.

Keeping a house, raising three kids, dealing with Big Bill and his black moods. He almost felt sorry for her.

Almost.

He finished dressing and walked back out to the car, hiking his pants up as he did.

"There's a coffee shop up ahead," Louis said when Liam slid into the front seat. "Let's go have a chat."

At the shop, Liam and Louis sat at a round wooden table while Aidan ordered their coffees. When he retrieved them from the barista and brought them over, Louis said, "First of all, I want you to know that in addition to Serrano, we have agents watching the house. So your clients are safe, for now."

"What do you mean, for now?" Liam asked.

"Let me give you some backstory," he said. "You know about the thousand missing people after the invasion of Cyprus, right?"

"Yahya mentioned it," Liam said. "And he told us there was a rumor that the bodies were buried at Gezi Park."

"That's correct. Our intelligence sources tell us the man responsible for that action was Cengiz Demir, a colonel in the MİT, the Turkish police. He's still with the service; he's now the head of the Directorate of Operations."

"From 1974?" Liam asked. "How old is he?"

"Seventy-five," Louis said. "He's a very important guy, and revealing his role in the operation would not only harm Turkey's relations with the West, but he himself could be charged with war crimes. So he has a powerful motivation to keep this information secret."

"And he has the resources to do so," Aidan said.

Louis nodded. "His unit collects information from covert sources in Turkey and abroad, including intelligence about drug trafficking, money laundering, and dealing in weapons. He has a network of operatives in and out of the country who report to him. We believe he's been manipulating the protests at Gezi Park to halt the construction and preserve his secret."

"If you already know all this, why can't the US government stop him?" Aidan asked.

"It's not that easy. Turkey is an important ally of ours in the Middle East, and we need a stable government there."

"How did Demir hear about the surveyor's report?" Liam asked.

"An informer in the building department saw the report and had it removed. There's no trace of it, and the surveyor, Musa Kemal, was brought into intelligence headquarters the same day for questioning. His body was found a couple of days later in an industrial park near the airport."

Liam remembered the hotel where they had stayed their last night in Istanbul—in that very neighborhood.

"We've been trying to trace copies of report," Louis said. "Our sources say Kemal insisted he had only made two copies—one for his records, one for the lead developer on the project, Ahmet Tikli."

"Yahya's friend," Aidan said. "The one who was killed."

"Correct. No one knows for sure what Tikli did with the report he received. He could have made many copies. We know he sent one package from his office the afternoon he died."

"To Yahya," Aidan said.

"The messenger company only had a street address for the delivery," Louis said. "We're assuming it went to Yahya. And he says he did receive a packet from Tikli with papers he was supposed to sign, and that a copy of the surveyor's report was tucked inside as well."

He picked up his coffee and sipped. "That night, after Tikli was shot to death in Gezi Park, someone broke into his office and ransacked it. We're assuming they took whatever copies of the report existed there, and that they also saw the messenger log. The next day, they questioned everyone in your cousin's office building."

"But he had already closed his office," Aidan said.

"Exactly. So they couldn't find anything. That night, they blew up the building, to be sure."

"These guys mean business," Liam said.

"You bet. Demir had evidence fabricated that the surveyor and the developer were laundering money to fund terrorist activities. That's how he explained both their deaths and all the affiliated actions. It's just luck that Mr. Farias didn't get caught quickly enough to be interrogated and then killed. But his luck may be about to run out."

"Why?" Aidan asked.

"Because in about two hours, Cengiz Demir will be landing at JFK."

24 – Holding Out

"You think Farias is holding back on us?" Liam asked. "He has before. And I don't trust him."

"I'm about ninety-nine percent certain Farias has something more to say," Louis said. "I didn't want to press him too much this morning, but I plan to dangle Demir's arrival in front of him and see how he reacts."

He looked at Liam. "You all right to go back to Basking Ridge, or you need to check in with your mother?"

"I left Ellen's car at her house." Liam sighed. "And I guess I ought to make sure my mom's all right before I run away again."

As he stood, he had to tug the stupid green pants up around his waist again; they'd slid down, exposing a line of his ass between them and the hem of the polo shirt. He was going to kill Louis Fleck when this was all over.

Louis drove them back to his house. "You want me to ride with you?" Aidan asked.

"You have some more intimate details of our sex life to share with my mom?" Liam said. "I think I can handle things myself from here. Don't start anything with Yahya until I get there, all right?"

"Will do," Louis said. Aidan climbed out of the backseat and got into the front beside Louis, and Liam watched them drive away. He felt in his pockets for the key to Ellen's car and realized he'd left it in his bedroom. Hell, he'd known he would have to see Doris again.

He walked up to the front porch and tried the front door. Locked. Again. Why hadn't he grabbed a house key before storming out earlier? He rapped on the door frame. "Ma! It's me."

The front door of the Damianis' house opened, and Frank Barrow stepped out onto his porch, wearing a pair of too-tight jeans and an untucked Hawaiian shirt that hung over his belly. "Your mom went off with your sister," he said. "I have a key, though."

It was just like his mother, Liam thought, to call the poor guy a fucking faggot but then take advantage of leaving a key with him. He knew the old house intimately, and he figured he could break in if he had to—but why go to the trouble? "Can I borrow the key?" he asked.

"Got it right here," Barrow said and pulled it slowly out of the front pocket of his jeans, keeping his eye on Liam. Liam had been in enough gay bars to recognize a stiff dick pressing against the fabric, even if Barrow hadn't pressed his other hand against his groin to make it pop.

It was such a blatant pass that Liam was tempted to laugh. Barrow walked down his steps and across the small lawn in front of both porches. The grass there was much better kept than in the rear; he figured that was Barrow's doing.

Barrow climbed the steps to Liam's porch. "I'd better hold onto this key," he said, as he moved past Liam on his way to the door. Liam was sure that the way Barrow's hand brushed against his crotch was no accident.

Barrow opened the front door and ushered Liam in ahead of

him. "I'm all right on my own," Liam said.

"You don't have to be," Barrow said, stepping in beside him and closing the door.

"Seriously," Liam said. "You can go."

"Doors in these houses don't lock automatically," Barrow said. "You have to turn the key. Wouldn't be right for me to leave Doris's house unlocked."

"Whatever," Liam said. He took the steps to the second floor two at a time the way he always had, and went into his room. He was gathering up his clothes when Barrow stepped into the doorway behind him.

"You must be really stressed out about your mom," he said. "I can help you relax."

"Thanks for the offer, but I've got a partner. He and I can relax just fine together." He bent over to pick up his shorts and jockstrap from the floor, and the green pants slid down, exposing his ass again.

As soon as he registered that, he felt Barrow's warm, damp hand on his naked butt. Barrow reached under the jockstrap and twisted, and Liam lost his patience.

He turned to face Barrow, grabbing the man's arm and turning it behind him. He got into the man's face, pressing his chest against Barrow's belly. "I said no," Liam said. "Now you can back away and retain the use of this arm, or…"

Face to face like that, Barrow was almost as tall as Aidan, and unexpectedly he leaned up and kissed Liam hard on the lips the way Aidan often did. Barrow shifted his posture, even with Liam restraining his arm, and pressed his erection against Liam's thigh. To his disgust, his dick responded.

He released Barrow's arm and backed away.

"You must be one horny bastard to keep after me when I said no."

"I've never been with a man like you," Barrow said, panting. "I could probably come just looking at you."

Maybe Aidan was right, and Liam really was an en exhibitionist. But then, what good was it having a body men wanted to worship if you never let them see it? He felt a kind of wild abandon and looked Barrow in the eyes. "Feel free," he said. "Because that's as close as you're going to get. I'll even help you along."

He stripped down, pulling off the too—tight polo shirt, the loose green pants and the thrift-store jockstrap. Then he turned his back to Barrow and, still naked, packed everything in the bag except the clothes he was going to wear.

He looked over at Barrow. He was groaning and jerking his dick so fast his hand was a blur. His eyes were wild, and it was even harder for Liam to resist sharing in the passion that welled up inside him. His dick was stiff and leaked precome, and it pronged away from his belly, the cowl sliding down.

Barrow yelped and shot a load onto the threadbare carpet. Liam and said, "I trust you'll clean up after yourself before you go." He quickly pulled on his jockstrap, shoving his still-stiff dick inside the pouch, then put on the rest of his clothes. Barrow stood there staring, the come still dribbling out of his dick.

Liam took one more look, then he went downstairs and out to Ellen's car. He jumped in and slammed the door, turned on the ignition, and pulled away from the curb before Barrow could come after him.

As he threaded his way through his hometown's narrow streets, he opened the windows to wipe any smell of sweat or semen away. Landmarks of his youth showed up, barely recognized—the middle school where he had first played baseball, the cemetery where his father was buried, the faux colonial Rutgers frat houses where he'd spied on older boys as a teenager.

He crossed the placid Raritan River on the Route 18 bridge, small boats bobbing at anchor, trees alongside the water in full leaf. Some college kids in bathing suits were joking around on the near shore.

He knew he ought to call his sisters and find out where his mother was, make sure she was all right, but for the moment he had to focus on Yahya Farias. What else was the man hiding? It wasn't his job to weasel out the truth; that was what Louis was for. And good luck to him, Liam thought.

There was an unfamiliar black car in the driveway when he parked. Because of the government plates, he assumed it belonged to the agent minding the clients. Louis's rental car was parked beside it.

Louis and the agent who'd met them at the airport, Serrano, answered the door. Liam followed them into the dining room, where Meryem, Yahya, and Aidan clustered with Ellen at the table around a laptop. She was explaining the advantages of different locations where the Fariases could live.

"Aidan, why don't you take Mrs. Farias and Mrs. Blattner outside?" Louis said. "Agent Serrano and I would like to have a few words with Mr. Farias."

"We'll finish this up later," Ellen said, closing the laptop. She and Meryem went out to the backyard, with Aidan to watch them. It was late afternoon by then, but the sun was still high in the sky, and the tall trees behind the house cast dark shadows over the lawn.

Louis sat across the dining room table from Yahya. Liam and Agent Serrano stood at the archway that led to the living room.

"I'll get right to the point, Mr. Farias," Louis said. "Cengiz Demir, one of the old guard of Turkish intelligence, is on his way here. I need to know why."

Yahya pulled a leather wallet from the pocket of his tan gabardine slacks and extracted a folded piece of paper from it. "He wants this," he said and handed it to Louis. "It is my copy of the surveyor's report."

"I thought you said this report was destroyed in the fire," Louis said.

Yahya shrugged. "I knew it was important, so I put a photocopy in the safe and kept the original with me. I thought I might need it for insurance."

25 – Drama Level

Liam's first reaction was vindication. He'd known Yahya Farias was holding something back, just hadn't known what. It made perfect sense, though. Farias was a sharp operator, and he must have expected that he'd need to keep a bargaining chip or two.

Liam was angry too; he didn't like it when clients kept secrets from him. He crossed his arms over his chest and glared at Farias, who had the sense to look sheepish.

Louis handed the form to Serrano, and Liam looked over his shoulder. Liam couldn't make any sense of it, because it was written in Turkish, but Serrano obviously could read the language. "It's what he says it is," the agent said.

Louis stood, and he and Agent Serrano walked into the living room to talk. Liam leaned backward so he could see out to the patio, and he motioned to Aidan to come in. Then he sat down at the armchair at the end of the table. He stared at Yahya but didn't say anything.

When Aidan came in, he slipped into a chair across from Yahya, then looked at Liam. "Mr. Farias has added an unexpected card to the game on the table," Liam said. "He had that surveyor's report with him all along."

"It is not that I did not trust you," Farias began, but Liam silenced him.

"It is what it is Now we figure out what happens next."

Liam hated to admit to a client that he wasn't in control of a situation. In this case, however, he had to cede control to the CIA. There was no way he was going up against them. "Our priority is protecting you and your family. That's what you hired us for, and we'll continue to do that until you no longer need us."

"But now that I have handed over the report," Yahya said, "what use am I to Demir? He should leave me alone."

"Demir is worried about more than a piece of paper," Aidan said. "He believes you know what's on that report, and why it matters. That makes you a threat to him, with or without the proof."

Louis and Serrano came back in then. "Where do we stand?" Liam asked.

"We're in a holding pattern right now, waiting for orders," Louis said.

"If the information in that report becomes public knowledge, that should protect Yahya, right?" Aidan asked. "Once he's no longer the only person who knows what Demir did, or has proof of it."

"Not necessarily," Serrano said. "Demir doesn't know Mr. Farias has given us the report—and even if he heard that, he might not believe it."

"I have some experience with men like Demir," Liam said. "At this point, he's angry, and quite possibly vindictive. This is a man who's accustomed to being in control, and you've snatched that away from him." As he spoke he recognized that he empathized somewhat with Demir, though for all the wrong reasons. "He could still come after Farias and his family, either to shut them up or to punish them."

"What if we leaked this information to a journalist?" Aidan said. "Agent Serrano, you speak Turkish. Don't you have a Turkish-speaking contact in the press who would love to get hold of this information? If this became public, then Demir would lose the backing of the government, right? He wouldn't have the resources to come after Yahya. He'd be too busy protecting himself."

"Hold on, Aidan," Louis said. "The decision to make this information public is going to come from way above us."

"But…" Aidan began, but Liam put his hand on his partner's arm.

"We'll talk about it later," Liam said. He was sure that Louis was constrained in what he could say by Agent Serrano's presence, and that they might get more out of him in private.

The doorbell rang, and everyone turned toward the front door. Liam stood and walked quickly to the front window. He tugged the drapes back with a finger and peered out. "Black sedan." He leaned farther around the curtain and caught sight of Teyze Eda and Aunt Sophia on the doorstep.

Ellen walked in from the patio, followed by Meryem. "Isn't someone going to answer the door?" She strode through the living room and opened the front door. "Mother," she said. "What are you doing here? I thought you and Teyze Eda were going to relax today."

"This gentleman believed we'd be safer here," Aunt Sophia said, motioning behind her to the limo driver from the day before. "I don't understand why, but as you can see, he had us pack for an overnight stay."

The two women walked in, and the driver followed with two roll-aboard-type bags. He nodded toward Serrano and backed out the door, closing it behind him.

Ellen turned to Serrano. "Are we all in danger?" she demanded. Liam could tell she was working up to a fight. He'd seen the same crossed arms and set chin in his partner.

"We're handling the situation," Serrano said.

"Why can't you take Yahya and his family to a secure location? This is my home, and I don't want it to become the scene of any international espionage. And I certainly don't want my children to get caught in the crossfire."

"There won't be any crossfire," Serrano said patiently. "And unfortunately, because the Fariases have been here with you since they arrived, your family is already involved."

"*Dame mazel y echa me a los perros,*" Teyze Eda said, and everyone looked at her. "Give me luck, and then throw me to the dogs." She smiled. "We Fariases have always been lucky. Now we trust to God. And we make dinner." She took her sister's hand, and they walked to the kitchen together.

Ellen looked from Serrano to Louis. No one said anything for a moment. "Fine," she said. "I'll have Daniel and Gil clean up the family room and make the sofa bed up. My mother and Teyze Eda can share."

Then she turned to Louis. "Of course, at least one of you is staying here too, right? You're not abandoning us."

"We have the house under surveillance," Serrano said. "Nobody is getting in or out of here unless we allow it."

"I'll stay here," Louis said. "Just give me a pillow and a place on the floor somewhere."

"He can stay in our room," Aidan said.

Liam glared at his partner. He had always looked forward to their time together before bed as a way to wind down, to share their experiences and plan their next day. Even though Louis was a friend, Liam didn't want him in the middle of their conversation. He and Aidan had a lot to talk about.

26 – Unknown Number

Aidan couldn't remember the last time he'd been jammed together with so many people in one house. Maybe a holiday dinner at Aunt Sophia's and Uncle Harold's? But then, everyone had gone home at the end of the day. And they'd been celebrating something, Thanksgiving or Hanukkah, a wedding or a bar mitzvah. Now wherever he turned, there was tension.

Ellen and Barry were upset that their hospitable impulse had turned dangerous. Their sons were already annoyed that the guests had put them out of their bedrooms, and when there was no room for them at the dining room table, they started to complain. Liam was in a funky mood, Louis was brooding, and Aidan didn't understand why Agent Serrano was still hanging around.

Yahya and Meryem didn't speak to each other except in monosyllables, and Havva and Ishak looked baffled. Only Aunt Sophia and Teyze Eda were in a good mood, happily cooking together.

Aidan volunteered to set up a table for himself and Liam, Havva and Ishak, and Ellen's kids outside. "We used to do this all the time as kids," he said to the Turks. "Aunt Sophia and Uncle Harold had huge family parties, and all the kids were sent to a separate table."

"We still do it," Ellen's oldest son, Daniel, said. "I'll get the folding table from the garage."

Aidan helped Daniel and Gil with the table and chairs. Havva and Ishak stood to the side, talking in low tones. Aidan was resentful that they didn't jump in to help, but Ishak did have a broken arm and they both had lots of their own family drama to deal with.

He understood Ellen was angry that her request for Aidan's help with her cousin had led to putting her family in danger, and worried that the situation was going to destroy his connection to the part of his family he was closest to.

He had always enjoyed those big family parties, getting to spend time with Ellen and her sister and all their other cousins. He missed that connection, living in Tunisia and then Nice, and he wanted to be sure it would continue.

Teyze Eda, Aunt Sophia, Meryem and Yahya, and Ellen and Barry sat at the dining room table, with the leaf pulled out to accommodate Agent Serrano and Louis Fleck. Aidan didn't envy them being stuck in the middle of the family drama, and was glad to sit outside with Liam, Havva and Ishak, and Ellen's sons.

The two sisters whipped up a traditional Turkish meal—eggplant roasted with peppers in a spicy tomato sauce, zucchini pancakes, and lamb chunks marinated in olive oil, milk, and onion, then grilled on shish kebab skewers. Ellen's boys turned up their noses at the food, but Aidan was determined to get them to try it, and by the end of the meal they were clamoring for more and asking why their grandmother didn't cook this kind of food more often.

Aidan quizzed them about school and Daniel's recent bar mitzvah. Ishak had heard tales of extravagant parties, and he wanted to hear all the details of food and decoration, which the boy hadn't noticed.

"I went to your mother's bat mitzvah, you know," Aidan said to them. "It was the first fancy one I ever went to. The theme was 'Up, Up, and Away,' and there were big balloons attached to baskets on each table."

"We had a basketball half-court," Daniel said. "My mom had the room decorated in red and blue, the colors of the Nets. They used to be in New Jersey, you know, before they moved to Brooklyn."

"They were in New York City before that," Aidan said.

"And all the kids got a basketball shirt that read *I scored a goal at Daniel's Bar Mitzvah*," Daniel continued, as if he hadn't heard Aidan at all.

"I'm sorry I missed it," Aidan said. "How old are you, Gil?"

"Eleven. But almost twelve. My mom already has the date for my bar mitzvah, next Halloween. My theme is going to be Gil's Candy Store, and the colors are going to be black and orange."

Havva and Ishak shook their heads at such oddity, but to Aidan it was all part of the family. His bar mitzvah, a month before Ellen's service, had been the last ordinary one in the family. No theme, no fancy album, no candle-lighting ceremony, entertainment, or special guests. He'd always felt like the poor relation because everything his cousins did was fancier, glitzier, or more expensive than what he did.

For dessert there were walnut baklava rolls topped with whipped cream, accompanied by tiny cups of sweet Turkish coffee. Daniel and Gil were excused to play video games. Aidan and Liam sat across from each other, but they didn't speak until Havva and Ishak had stood to walk to the edge of the yard and smoke cigarettes.

"You're really on edge," Aidan said to Liam. "What's up?"

"I'm fine. Just watchful."

"I've seen you watchful. This is something more. Is it your mother?"

"It's nothing, Aidan. All right?"

Aidan crossed his arms over his chest. "Fine."

Liam sighed. "You know that guy on the porch next to my mother's?" he asked, and for a moment Aidan was confused.

"Oh, yeah. What about him?"

"He propositioned me."

"So? You're gorgeous. You get propositioned all the time."

"When I went back yesterday, I didn't have a key to the house, so Frank came over and let me in."

Aidan pulled back. "You are NOT going to tell me you fucked him, are you?"

"Of course not," Liam said. "I'm not a whore."

"But," Aidan said.

"But he said that I turned him on, and that he could come just from watching me. So I let him."

"What do you mean, you let him?"

"I mean I fiddled around in my room naked, and he jerked himself off while he watched me."

Aidan couldn't help bursting into laughter. "My big porn star," he said, and he put his arm around Liam. "If the bodyguard business ever slows down, we can get you one of those webcam channels."

"I'm serious, Aidan," Liam said, pushing him away. "It was kind of creepy. And I shouldn't have done it. What if I'd lost control and done something more? Something that I'd hate and regret and that would hurt you?"

Aidan took a deep breath. "Here's the thing, sweetheart. I know you. And I know you never lose control."

"I do. Look at the way I yelled at Yahya and Ishak when they were arguing. And you should have seen me with my mom. Totally lost it."

"Fine. You can run amok sometimes. And if you had done something with this guy, it would have been a problem. I won't lie to you. But whatever happens between us, whether you get carried away or I do, we'll work it out, because we love each other, and love is the most powerful weapon in the world."

He watched Liam's face as he processed all that information.

"I'm glad you told me," Aidan said. "Secrets can be toxic. Look at all the problems the Fariases have gone through because of the secrets they've been keeping."

"How did I get so lucky?" Liam asked. He reached out for Aidan's hand, and squeezed.

"Because for a change, the universe gave us both what we deserved," Aidan said.

Serrano finally left, after assuring them all that there would be agents watching the house overnight. Aunt Sophia and Teyze Eda went to bed early. Ellen and Barry retreated to their room, as did Meryem and Yahya, and Havva and Ishak. Aidan figured there were going to be a lot of heated conversations going on in private that night.

That left Aidan, Liam, and Louis in the living room. "Can I go for a walk around the property?" Liam asked Louis. "Or will a couple of agents with Uzis jump up to greet me?"

"We don't use Uzis," Louis said. "But I think we're all fine staying inside."

It was only nine o'clock, but Aidan was tired. "I say we go to bed," he said.

"I can sleep down here," Louis said.

"No, Gil has an extra sleeping bag. He left it in our room for you." They were staying in Gil's room, with its twin beds on opposite sides. When they got upstairs, they found that Gil had unrolled the bag in the middle of the room with a pillow at the head.

"I don't want to come between you two," Louis said, only half joking.

"It'll be like a sleepover," Aidan said.

"Never did one of those," Liam said.

Aidan and Louis looked at him. "Never?"

"If you sleep over at somebody's house, you've got to invite them back to yours, right?" Liam asked.

They both nodded.

"Not happening in my house," Liam said. "I'm going to the bathroom."

"What crawled up his ass and died?" Louis asked when Liam had left the room.

"Must be something connected with his mother, don't you

think? Even though he says it's not."

"Families are weird," Louis said.

When they were all done with the bathroom and the lights were out, Louis said, "Good night, John Boy."

Liam answered, "Good night, Mary Ellen."

Aidan said, "Excuse me? Is that some kind of code?"

"It's from an old TV program, *The Waltons*," Louis said. "At the end of each episode the lights in the house would wink out, one by one, and the characters would say good night to each other."

"Sounds very gay," Aidan said.

"Then I'm stunned you don't know about it," Liam said, and Louis snorted with laughter.

Sunday morning, Aidan awoke to the sound of water running in pipes and the smell of bacon frying. Louis was snoring lightly on the floor, and Liam was sitting up on his bed, checking e-mail on his phone.

"Morning," Aidan said in a low voice. "You feeling better?"

"I'm fine, Aidan."

Louis rolled onto his back, and the sound of his snoring increased, waking him up. "Happy, joy," he said and stretched his arms.

Aidan slept in the nude; he pulled his boxers on under the covers, oddly shy in front of Louis, and then went to the bathroom. Eventually the three of them ended up downstairs in the kitchen, where Aunt Sophia was managing an assembly line of breakfast foods. She and her sister worked so smoothly together you'd never think they had been separated for decades.

"My sister says that our parents are buried not far away," Teyze Eda said to Aidan. "Will we be able to go there to see them?"

"Not today," Louis said. "We need you all to stay together."

"My boys have to go to school tomorrow," Ellen said. "And Barry has to go to work. Our lives can't just stop."

"I hope to have some answers for you today," Louis said.

Ellen did not appear satisfied with that answer, and Aidan was glad she was focusing her irritation on Louis rather than on himself and Liam, as usually happened when they had to restrict the movements of clients.

They ate in shifts in the kitchen and the dining room. Aidan and Havva volunteered to do the dishes, and while they worked, the rest of the family gathered in small groups in different parts of the house. Aidan worried about how they'd all be behaving by the end of a day of forced intimacy.

Havva finished loading the dishwasher, and Aidan showed her how to turn it on. "How are you guys holding up?" he asked her.

"I hope we will be in our own home soon," she said.

"You will be. Louis is a good guy; he'll take care of your family."

"He will do what is best for your country," she said. "Not for us."

"Then Liam and I will look out for you."

She leaned up and kissed him on the cheek. "You are a good man, Aidan. I hope Ishak finds someone like you or Liam."

As they walked into the living room, Aidan heard strange music and realized it was Yahya's cell phone ringing. "Who is calling me?" he asked. "I don't know this number."

Louis stepped close to him. "Answer it."

Yahya answered, then carried on a heated conversation in Turkish. Aidan couldn't make out a bit of it, and from the look on Liam's face, he could tell his partner couldn't either.

Yahya said something abruptly and then ended the call. His face was pale, and his hand shook. "Was Demir," he said. "He wishes to meet with me, give me money in exchange for the report I have. I do not believe him. I tell him no."

27 – True Self

Aidan was stunned. That wasn't the reaction they had expected from Cengiz Demir. Ambush, arson, gunfire—but negotiation?

He looked to Liam, who appeared as startled as he was. Ellen and Aunt Sophia sat in a corner of the living room, their attention focused on Yahya as well.

Louis said, "Let me call Serrano," and walked out to the backyard.

"You think I am wrong?" Yahya asked Liam and Aidan.

"You probably should have stalled him," Liam said. "Give the agents a chance to make some arrangements."

"I do not trust anyone," Yahya said. He crossed his arms over his chest.

"Then how do you expect to get out of this mess?" Ellen demanded. "You can't stay here forever with my family as hostages."

"Yahya and Meryem and their children are our family," Aunt Sophia said. "We will do whatever we can to help them." She took her daughter's hand and squeezed.

As Yahya began to pace around the living room, Aidan caught Liam's eye, and they stepped toward the dining room. "What do you think is up?" Aidan asked in a low voice.

"Could be a trap," Liam said. "Or it could be a legitimate attempt. Demir has to get that proof back from Yahya. He's tried to get it by force. This could be his only chance to save himself.

Negotiation is the last resort of the cornered man who wants to stay alive."

"Is that a quote?"

"Sure. I just said it."

Aidan elbowed him as Louis came inside. Ishak, Meryem, and Havva followed him. "Can you call Demir back?" Louis asked Yahya.

"Why?"

"We think the best thing to do would be to arrange a meeting. Someone high up in the Agency has spoken to a counterpart at the Turkish MİT—someone higher than Demir. They would like the opportunity to take him home for questioning."

"Why does Mr. Farias have to be involved?" Liam asked.

Louis turned to him. "Demir appears to have gone rogue, with the help of one or more of his loyal operatives stationed in New York. His own people don't know where he is or how to contact him. They need our help to rope him in."

The four Fariases clustered together, talking rapidly in Turkish, as Liam and Louis debated how a meeting could be arranged with minimal risk to Yahya.

Aidan had an idea. He pulled his cell phone out of his pocket and did a quick Internet search for the cemetery where his grandparents were buried. He'd been there a few times as a teenager and adult, to visit their graves, and he was pretty certain Aunt Sophia's parents were there as well.

The cemetery was a huge property at the intersection of Routes 1 and 9 in Woodbridge. He came up with the name and looked at his partner. Liam was still arguing with Louis.

"I have an idea," Aidan said. "Suppose we meet them at Beth Shalom Cemetery in Woodbridge?" He looked at Aunt Sophia. "That's where your parents are, right? And my Nana Rose and my grandfather."

She nodded.

Aidan turned back to Liam and Louis. "It's a big, flat area, lots of visibility. And with the black cars you guys drive, you could have agents stationed around the area looking like mourners."

"I don't like the idea of such a public place," Louis said. "Too much opportunity for bystanders to get in the way."

"You could cordon off part of the grounds," Aidan said. "Make it look like a celebrity funeral, for example. Have agents stationed to keep people away. Give them earpieces to make them look official, and people will listen to them."

"Our agents don't need earpieces to look official," Louis said.

"I agree with Aidan," Liam said. "A cemetery is a great place for a meeting. Visibility, security."

Louis thought about it for a moment, then turned to Yahya. "How about you, Mr. Farias? You willing to go through with this?"

"I will do it," Ishak said. He stood, and Aidan thought he saw something different in the younger man's posture, something more confident and assertive than he had seen before.

Everyone turned to look at Ishak. "If I am dressed as a woman, no one will notice me at first. I can show the paper somehow and lure this man out to receive it. Then he can be arrested."

"No," Meryem said, shaking her head. "Not you."

"Yes, me." Ishak looked at his parents. "I know what you think of me, that I am weak and foolish. But I am not. I am strong, and I have courage."

Aidan admired Ishak for speaking up. "I think it's a great idea," he said, warming to the idea. "We can stage a fake unveiling, which will give us a reason to have a large group of people around one of the graves. Yahya makes a plan to meet Demir nearby."

He turned to Ishak. "I'll bet you'd look great in black. A long dress, a veil over your head. At first you'll look like one of the mourners, moving away from the crowd to get some space. You can pull out the paper and hold it up. Louis will have people covering you until Demir shows his face. Then the Turks can arrest him."

Liam looked at Aidan. "That's a good plan. Demir will be expecting Yahya, so a woman will throw him off guard."

"Let me see what I can do," Louis said and went back outside.

"I don't understand," Aunt Sophia said. "Why would Ishak dress as a woman?"

Meryem began to explain to her, and Liam pulled Aidan aside. "Tell me what this unveiling thing is."

"It's a ceremony, usually a year after a person dies, when the family gathers at the grave. By then the tombstone has been put in place, and the cemetery puts a sheet over it, to be revealed during the ceremony."

"So they have these things all the time? It's not something that will attract a lot of attention?"

"All the time. Though sometimes if the person dies in the winter, they don't wait a full year for the unveiling—they do it while the weather's still warm."

"You come from a practical people," Liam said drily.

Louis came back in with the authorization to proceed, and Serrano arrived a few minutes later. Yahya opened his phone and dialed the number Demir had used. Serrano coached Yahya to arrange the meeting, that afternoon at the cemetery.

The conversation was all in Turkish, so Aidan couldn't understand any of it. But from Yahya's body language, he could tell that the man was a born negotiator. Yahya kept repeating some of the same phrases, shaking his head, until finally he nodded, and the tenor of his voice changed. He ended the call and looked at them.

"He does not want to do what I tell him, but I keep him arguing and negotiating. I tell him the only way I will meet him is at the grave of my grandfather. That my *dede's* spirit will protect me." He looked at Ishak. "What I mean is that my dede and all my ancestors will protect my son as he does this dangerous thing."

He opened his arms, and Ishak stepped up and hugged him. Then Meryem and Havva joined the group hug, all of them smiling and crying at the same time.

"All right, we've got a lot to do, and not much time," Louis said. It was close to ten o'clock then, and Yahya had arranged to meet Demir at three o'clock that afternoon.

"I can drive Havva and Ishak back to the mall to find the right clothes," Aidan volunteered.

Louis shook his head. "I'll get an agent to drive you."

Aidan turned to Aunt Sophia. "Can you go over to the cemetery with Louis and show him where your parents are buried? Ellen, you could talk to the cemetery people. You know what kind of stuff they'll need—the sheet over the tombstone, the chairs, and all."

"Feel free to take over, Aidan," Louis said, but he smiled.

"Welcome to my world," Liam said. "Have an assignment for me, boss?"

"Can you get aerial photos of the cemetery online?" He turned to Louis. "You guys must have a tactical specialist. Liam can help him find the best defensive positions and work out the choreography."

Within a half hour, a female agent named Debra Lan was there to take Aidan, Havva, and Ishak to the mall to shop. "I saw the perfect store," Havva said as they drove. "They had beautiful dresses, just right for my brother."

They arrived as the mall was opening, and Havva swept in with Ishak, Aidan, and Agent Lan following in her wake. She opened her purse and handed a piece of paper to Aidan and a credit card. "Makeup from Sephora," she said. "It's down the hall to the right, then around the corner. Ask someone to help you. Make sure you get the right shades."

"Yes, ma'am," Aidan said and saluted. Then Havva led her brother and Agent Lan toward the boutique she'd noticed. When Aidan joined them there with the cosmetics, Ishak was modeling a slinky black dress. "You see the high neck, to cover this," Havva said to Aidan, running her finger over her throat where Ishak's Adam's apple was.

She put her hands on her hips. "Yes, the dress is perfect. What do you think, Ishak?"

"It is fine. But what about my hair? All my beautiful wigs were burned." His dark hair was cut boyishly short.

"I saw a wig kiosk on my way back from Sephora," Aidan said. They paid for the dress, then headed to a shoe store. While Aidan found black dress shoes for himself and Liam, Ishak picked through a half dozen pairs of black shoes. "Nothing with too high a heel," Aidan said. "Remember, you're going to be walking on rough ground."

He detoured back to the Gap for black slacks and white shirts for himself and Liam, while Havva took Ishak to the wig kiosk, where he ended up with a dark wig with bangs.

Havva picked up a few other items for her parents and her grandmother for the ceremony; then they all traveled back to Basking Ridge with Agent Lan. By the time they arrived, Louis had returned from the cemetery with his contingent, and the arrangements had all been made for the fake unveiling. Liam and Agent Serrano had gone over the aerial photographs of the cemetery. Other agents had liaised with local law enforcement and Turkish intelligence. Louis had commandeered an easel that Daniel used for watercolors and drawn up complicated maps and lists of instructions. It was like walking into the operations center for a battle, cunningly hidden inside a suburban mini-mansion.

By two thirty, two limousines arrived at the Blattner house to chauffeur the family to the cemetery. Barry and his boys had yarmulkes for all the men and lacy circles for the women to wear on their heads. Barry was going to pretend to be the rabbi, and he carried a white fringed prayer shawl over his arm along with a large black Bible.

Ishak made a very convincing woman, Aidan thought as they all walked outside. He carried himself well in the stylish knee-length black dress his sister had picked out for him, with a black silk pashmina to cover the cast on his arm. Everyone else had dressed in their best clothes, even the two boys, Daniel and Gil. Ellen had resisted having them go, but they'd wanted to be part of the event, and Louis assured her that they'd be safe, and that the presence of kids would add realism to the scene.

Liam and Aidan conferred as the family began to get into the limo. "There are going to be agents in place all around us at the cemetery," Liam said in a low voice. "But we have to remember our primary job is to keep the Fariases safe."

"Not just them," Aidan said.

"Right now, Yahya is the one who's paying the bills," Liam said. "And he's going to be the primary target. So we both keep an eye on him, and we trust Louis's people to do their part."

Serrano accompanied the Blattners and the two grandmothers in one limo, along with a couple of other agents in dark suits. Liam, Aidan, and Louis joined the Fariases in the other. Across from Aidan, Ishak shifted position to accommodate his cast as well as the folds of his black dress. "You all right?" Aidan asked him.

"I am excited," he said. "To show my parents my true self."

Meryem said, "I know your true self, Ishak. You do not need to do this."

He said something to her in Turkish that Aidan assumed was to be reassuring, and then no one spoke for the rest of the ride to the cemetery.

28 – Live in Your Heart

Despite his familiarity with the aerial photographs, Liam was surprised at how large the cemetery was, and how varied. Near the entrance, low roofs sheltered what looked like condos for the dead—long stacks of boxes that resembled mailboxes at gated communities, though in this case each box was large enough to slide in a coffin and had a marble face engraved with inscriptions in English and Hebrew.

A cluster of family pavilions, some in classical style, others modern. Several sections had upright tombstones, while others had flat stones inset into the ground. The limo drove around a long, winding path, stopping near where a green canopy had been set up over a grave. A white cloth had been laid over a tombstone.

He'd never been to a Jewish funeral, so he was uncertain of the protocol, but he trusted Aidan to make sure he didn't demonstrate his ignorance. He looked around the cemetery; there was another tent set up in a different section, with an open grave, though there was no one around it.

A few other cars were scattered around the property. Liam visualized the map in his brain and identified which belonged to agents. He and Serrano had done a good job, he thought. All the sight lines were covered, and the perimeter security would prevent unauthorized people from getting through. All the agents had photos of Demir and instructions not to impede him or anyone with him unless things turned ugly.

Liam climbed out of the limo and held the door for the rest of the passengers. They joined the Blattners to walk toward the green awning. They had chosen this particular site for the unveiling because of its logistics. The names on the tombstones were all Jewish in origin—Edelman, Rifkin, Leibowitz. "Where's your family plot?" he whispered to Aidan.

"Down the hill, in a section called Mount of Olives. That's the name of a big cemetery in Jerusalem. Each one of the sections here belongs to a different congregation, some Orthodox, some Conservative, some Reformed."

Liam noted the irregular pattern of the tombstones—some were double, for husband and wife. Others were single stones, and one had been carved in the shape of a tree trunk, with no branches and a flat top. There was a proliferation of Hebrew letters, and the occasional Jewish star, pair of tablets, or, oddly, pairs of splayed hands.

He was sure Aidan knew all about it. Not because he was Jewish, but because that was the kind of arcane trivia his partner loved.

Barry pulled on his prayer shawl and led the group of ersatz mourners toward the grave, where they clustered under the awning and took seats on the folding chairs. Liam and Aidan stayed close to the Fariases, and he also kept an eye on Louis, who had an earpiece so he could communicate with the other agents.

Barry stepped up to the grave and began reading a prayer in Hebrew. Louis looked at Liam and nodded slightly to the left. A few hundred yards away, another black car had pulled up in front of an ornate wrought-iron gate leading into another congregation's burial site.

Liam stepped close to Louis. "We think that's Demir," Louis whispered. "Can't be sure until he gets out of the car."

Louis reached out and tapped Ishak on his good arm. "You sure you want to do this?" he asked. "There's no shame in backing out now. We can surround the car, and you don't have to do anything."

"You cannot be sure it is Demir until he steps outside," Ishak said. "I heard you. So I must do this."

"There's a sniper behind one of the tombstones to your right," Louis said. "If you hear any gunfire, just hit the ground, all right?"

"I will."

Liam couldn't help but admire Ishak's regal posture as he struck out across the grass toward the graves of his great-grandparents. He clutched a black prayer book in his hands; the original copy of the report the building surveyor had prepared was tucked inside.

The air around Liam crackled with tension as everyone pretended to look at the grave, but Liam, Aidan, and Louis all had their eyes on Ishak. Liam hated sending a young client out like that on his own, so unprotected and exposed, but it was the way things had to work.

Ishak stumbled on a rough piece of ground, his good arm flailing for balance, but righted himself. He crossed the street walked among the tombstones, peering at the names. He stopped at one marble slab, then bent down and picked up a pair of pebbles from the ground. He placed one on each side of the top of the stone.

"Do you think that's a signal?" Liam whispered to Aidan.

Aidan shook his head. "It's the custom. Kind of like leaving a calling card for the dead."

"There's no movement," Louis said to someone on his communication network. "Is that really Demir in the car?"

Liam couldn't tell if Louis got a response. Ishak looked around, then dramatically drew the piece of paper from the prayer book. He shook it out, and it fluttered in the light breeze. Then he put it on top of the tombstone, anchored by the pebbles there.

He leaned down and kissed the stone, then stood and began to walk slowly back toward the family. When he got to the street, though, he turned and continued up toward the car they thought held Cengiz Demir.

"That's not part of the program," Louis muttered. "What the fuck does he think he's doing?"

"I'll get him," Liam said and started forward.

Louis grabbed his arm. "Give him a minute."

"He could be in danger, Louis. I'm supposed to protect him."

Before Liam could leave the tent, Ishak reached the car and rapped sharply on the windshield. Louis listened to something on his earpiece and then muttered, "Sniper is ready," to Liam.

The door opened on the passenger side, and a white-haired man in a dark business suit stepped out of the car. His tanned face, even at this distance, was laced with lines, and a scar crossed his forehead. "Do we have an ID?" Louis asked.

The driver's door opened as well, and a younger man stepped out holding a handgun aimed at Ishak. They couldn't hear what was said between Ishak and the older man, but as soon as the man turned and the agents could see his profile, Agent Serrano stepped out from under the canopy and shouted something in Turkish.

The older man tried to grab Ishak and use him as a shield, but it looked like Ishak kneed him in the balls, and he doubled over. Very quickly there were agents everywhere, and the driver was disarmed.

An SUV pulled up behind Demir's car, and several coffee-colored men in suits tumbled out. Liam strode across to Ishak, took his good arm, and led him back to the canopy, where his family waited for him, all of them corralled by Aidan and Louis.

"You were so brave!" Havva said, wrapping her arms around her brother.

"But so foolish!" Meryem said. Liam saw that she was crying. She hugged her son too, and then he turned to his father.

"My son has the courage of a lion," Yahya said. He leaned forward and kissed Ishak gently on both cheeks. "I am very proud of you."

Ishak pulled a tissue from his pocket and dabbed at his mascara.

The men from the SUV bundled Demir and his driver into their vehicle. One of them drove Demir's car, and the SUV followed it down the winding path and out of the cemetery.

"And now," Teyze Eda said. "I would like to see the graves of my parents."

Agent Serrano joined them as they walked toward the graves. "Thank you very much for your assistance," he said to Ishak. "You are very cool under pressure. You'd make a good undercover agent."

"Thank you," Ishak said. "But I prefer to do something that does not disturb my makeup."

Liam almost thought Ishak winked.

"You should all be safe now," Serrano said. "The Turks have Demir, as well as the building inspector's report. Now it's up to them to decide what to do." He shook hands with everyone, then left with another agent.

Liam and Aidan waited while the family gathered around the graves of Aunt Sophia's and Teyze Eda's parents. "You don't want to join them?" Liam asked.

Aidan shook his head. "Other side of the family. I'm related to them through Aunt Sophia's husband, my father's brother. But I would like to find my grandparents. Aaron and Rose Greene. The last time I was here was with my parents, a year before my mom died, so I don't remember exactly where they are, but I remember the section is called Mount Tabor."

"I saw that on the map," Liam said. "It's down the hill, this way." He began to lead, and Aidan hurried to catch up with him.

"You don't have to come with me," his partner said.

"Sure I do."

They walked up to a wrought-iron fence segregating one area of the cemetery from the rest. There were Hebrew letters on an arched gate that led inside.

"I'll take this side; you take that one," Liam said. He walked between the graves, scanning the tombstones, not finding anything. He looked up to see Aidan across from him, standing beside a tall marble tombstone. From his posture it looked like he was crying.

Liam strode across the rows of graves, stumbling once, but determined to get to his partner. Aidan looked up at him with tears streaking his cheeks, and Liam wrapped him in an embrace.

"I didn't realize you were so close to your grandparents," he said into his partner's hair.

"I never knew my grandfather," Aidan said, sniffling. "He died before I was born. And my Nana Rose was kind of a cold fish, if you want to know the truth. Uncle Harold was her favorite, not my father, so she spent a lot more time with Ellen and her sister than with me. But they're all gone now. My parents and both sets of grandparents. It's just me. I can say the Kaddish prayer for them all—but who'll say it for me? Who'll mourn me when I'm gone?"

He was crying again, and Liam leaned down and kissed the top of his head. "You aren't alone, Aidan," he said. "As long as I'm alive, you'll never be. And if something happens to you, and I'm still here, and you want me to say a million prayers for you, you let me know."

Aidan pulled a tissue from his back pocket and dried his eyes. "I love you, Liam."

"I love you too, sweetheart. And I always will."

Aidan looked up at him, and the depth of emotion in his partner's eyes rocked Liam's world. With Aidan by his side, he thought he could face anything.

"Will you come back with me to my mother's?" he asked. "I need to make sure she's all right before we go back to France."

"I will live in your heart, die in your lap, and be buried in your eyes—and what's more, I will go with you to your mother's."

"Somehow, I have a feeling that's a quote," Liam said. "You can tell me where it's from on the way there." Though he usually didn't care for public display of emotion, he took Aidan's hand, and they walked back to the family hand in hand.

29 – TOGETHER

Aidan was surprised at how affected he'd been at his grandparents' grave. But being there reminded him of all he'd lost, and it overwhelmed him. He'd never thought too much about having children, but suddenly, standing there at the grave, he had a sense of how many generations of his family had struggled so that he could carry on the traditions his people had cherished for thousands of years.

As they rode back to Ellen's house in the limo, he thought about what Liam had said. That if Aidan went first, he would say whatever prayers Aidan wanted. But Aidan couldn't see his tall, blond partner standing at a grave site, reciting the Mourner's Kaddish, lighting a candle in his memory every year on the anniversary of his death. Yes, Liam would mourn him, in his own way. But it wasn't the same as having a child to say those prayers, as he did for his parents, as they had done for theirs, back for generations.

Had he let his people down in some way, he wondered? By not being religious enough, by dating outside his faith, by not having children to carry on his genetic material? He had tried, in his way, to be a good Jew. He remembered learning in Sunday school that Rabbi Hillel, when asked to explain the essence of Judaism while standing on one foot, had said simply, *"Love thy neighbor as thyself."* He had taken that as his own motto.

As a teacher, and as a bodyguard, his mission had been to help others. With Liam by his side, he hoped he could continue to do that.

He looked across the limo seat to where his partner stared out at the passing countryside. Liam had always been so strong for him; it was time for him to return the favor, to give up wallowing in sadness and be the partner Liam needed him to be.

When they got back to Ellen's house, Louis thanked the Fariases and the Blattners and then walked over to Liam and Aidan. "I'm glad everything worked out," Louis said.

"Thanks for all your help," Liam said. "Couldn't have done it without you."

"I'm heading down to Baltimore," Louis said. "Taking a couple of personal days to hang with the homeys. But I'll be back in Nice by the end of the week."

Liam held out his hand, and Louis shook it. "Have a good trip." Liam turned to Aidan. "I'm going to change and see if I can get a workout in before we go over to my mother's."

He left, and Louis said, "You take care of the big lug, all right? This stuff with his mother bothers him more than he lets on."

"I will." Aidan hugged Louis. "We'll all get together for dinner soon."

"Hassan would like that."

After Louis left, Aidan found Yahya and Meryem in the living room with Ellen and Barry. "Liam and I are going to head out soon," Aidan said. "Ellen, could we borrow your extra car for a day or two? We'll get it back to you before we fly out."

"No problem," Ellen said.

Barry shook his head. "Is this what you guys do all the time?

What went down today?"

"Most of the time our work is very mundane," Aidan said. "We chaperone tourists. We stand around outside hotel rooms. It very rarely gets dangerous."

"Still. Makes me glad I work on Wall Street."

"You will go back to France now?" Yahya asked.

Aidan nodded. "In the next day or two. Liam has some stuff to resolve with his mother."

"I must pay you."

"The Agence will bill you," Aidan said. "However you worked things out with them."

"We owe you a great deal," Meryem said. She stood to embrace him. "Thank you for everything." Then she whispered in his ear, "And for bringing my husband and my son together."

Aidan went upstairs to pack their gear, assuming either they'd stay over with Liam's mother or at a motel somewhere. There was a surprising amount to pack, considering all they'd lost back in Istanbul, but stuff had a habit of accumulating on you—all the duty-free and mall purchases, including a new duffle to carry it all in.

He carried the bags downstairs. "You leaving now, cuz?" Ellen said, coming out of the kitchen.

"Once Liam finishes his workout."

"It's certainly been an eventful visit," she said. "Listen, I've been doing some work with a client based in Paris. Barry and I were thinking of taking a trip there."

"Can you make a side trip to the Riviera?" Aidan asked. "Or

maybe Liam and I can fly up to Paris and see you."

"We'll work something out." She hugged him. "I was probably a real bitch yesterday. I'm sorry."

"No hurt feelings," Aidan said. "I love a woman who protects her family."

"And you're part of that family," she said. "Don't you ever forget."

"I won't."

Aidan found Liam out in the backyard, doing jumping jacks. Havva and Ishak were lounging on chaises, alternately chatting and watching him. "That's my Liam," Aidan said, sitting beside them. "Loves an audience."

"And we both enjoy the show," Havva said.

Aidan noticed Ishak had changed out of his black dress into a pair of shorts and a tank top. "What are you both going to do now?" he asked.

"I begin studying for the New York bar exam," Havva said. "Soon I hope to be an attorney here."

Aidan turned to Ishak. "And you?"

"My father wishes to buy some property," he said. "I will work with him."

Aidan's eyebrows rose. "Really?"

"I will study design at the same time. Maybe we will help each other." He smiled mischievously.

"Maybe so."

Liam's phone rang, and Aidan grabbed it from the table while

Liam continued his push-ups.

"Hello?"

"Billy, it's Jeannie. You've got to get over here. Enzo's been drinking, and he's going nuts again."

"Where are you?"

"Is this Billy?"

"It's Aidan. His partner. Where are you, Jeannie? At your mom's house?"

"Yeah. Can you get here quick?"

"Quick as we can," Aidan said and hung up.

30 – Reality Show

"I'm going to kill him," Liam said, his hands clenched around the steering wheel. He was sure he stunk after his workout, but he didn't want to waste time showering.

"You're not going to kill him," Aidan said. "Maybe you'll break a body part or two. But if you kill him, you'll go to jail. And I don't want to be jealous of your cell mate."

Liam stopped the car in front of his mother's house and jumped out, then stalked up to the front door. If it wasn't unlocked, he was going to kick it in. Just a warm-up for what he planned for Enzo.

Frank Barrow was on his porch next door. He called hello and waved, but Liam ignored him. He tried the handle, and the door was unlocked. "Jeannie!" he bellowed as he walked inside.

He heard her in the kitchen, at the back of the house. "Enzo, go!" she said. She was pushing him toward the back door as Liam entered the room.

"Hold it right there, asshole!" he yelled, but Enzo was out the door.

Jeannie tried to grab Liam's arm, but he shook her off as he pushed past. All the rage he'd been feeling for the past week had bubbled up inside, and he wanted nothing more than to beat that bastard Enzo within an inch of his life.

When he got outside, he saw Enzo hotfooting it through the ratty backyard, heading for the gate in the rickety wooden fence. He jumped down the couple of steps to the ground and lit out for Enzo, catching him at the gate, where a rusty padlock kept it shut. Enzo was slamming the gate, and when he turned to face Liam, he looked panicked.

Liam hit him first in the soft flab of his stomach. Enzo woofed out a breath and doubled over. Liam kept punching him as he began to bleed and cry.

"Billy, get off him!" Jeannie was behind him, tugging on his shirt.

Doris opened the upstairs window and leaned outside. "Kill the bastard, Billy!"

For once in his life, Liam wanted to do exactly what his mother asked. He reached back to slug Enzo again, but someone grabbed his arm.

"Enough, Liam!" Aidan said.

Liam shook him off without a word, and instead of hitting Enzo, he kneed the man in the groin. Enzo fell to the ground, but before Liam could haul him up and continue the beating, Aidan got him in a headlock.

He twisted his way free, sweating, his heart beating fast, ready to knock Aidan on his ass for interfering.

"No more!" Aidan said. "You made your point."

"You bastard!" Jeannie screamed. "You hurt Enzo!"

She tried to rush at Liam, but Aidan released his hold on his partner and backhanded Jeannie against her cheek. "Liam will never hit you because you're his sister," Aidan said. "But that doesn't matter to me."

She staggered backward, holding her hand against her cheek. From the upstairs window, Doris cheered.

Liam looked around. Enzo was sprawled on the ground, blood leaking from the corner of his mouth. Jeannie stood stunned from Aidan's smack, her cheek already beginning to blossom red. Aidan looked as determined as Liam had ever seen him, his jaw set and his fists up in a defensive stance Liam recognized he'd taught him.

From his kitchen window, overlooking the yard, Frank Barrow said, "You guys are better than any reality show on TV."

"Yeah, call this one *Why I Left Jersey*," Liam said. He turned and stalked into the kitchen, where he stopped at the sink to wash his hands.

"You all right?" Aidan asked from behind him.

Liam thought about it as the hot water ran over his hands and pooled pink around the drain. "You know, I haven't hit my sister since we were kids," he said. "Maybe if I'd knocked her around more, she'd have turned out better."

From upstairs he heard a heavy thumping, what sounded like his mother banging against the floor or the wall. He looked out the window and saw Jeannie sitting on the ground next to Enzo, his head against her breast. "I'd better see what the old bitch wants."

He walked out to the living room, with Aidan behind him, and discovered that the thumping noise was Doris coming down the stairs from the second floor, banging a metal cane on each riser.

"Ma, you shouldn't be out of bed," Liam said.

"You reminded me of your father out there," Doris said, and Liam was surprised to see that she was smiling. How could any memory of Big Bill be a good one?

She thumped down the last two steps and sat down hard in a faded wing chair with a torn fringe at the bottom. "I ever tell you I had two sweethearts, back before I got married? One was your dad. The other was Sandro Battaglione."

Liam stared at her. "Battaglione? Related to Enzo?"

"His father. My own pop, he hated both of them. 'A wop and a mick,' he called 'em." Doris's maiden name had been Erickson, Liam remembered. Her mother was German, her father Danish. And apparently just as much of a prick as Big Bill.

"One Saturday night, I went to a dance with Sandro. Bill got drunk and waited for us to come out. Then he walloped Sandro, like you did with Enzo." She cackled with laughter. "He grabbed my arm and dragged me to his car, leaving Sandro lying there outside the hall. We got into the backseat, and we made you that very night."

Liam couldn't decide which grossed him out more—hearing about his own conception, or considering how much like his father he was.

The kitchen door banged open, and Liam heard Enzo and Jeannie talking. "I should get out of here," he said.

"Oh, don't be such a big baby," Doris said. She cackled again. "I gotta tell you, in addition to the fight, one of the things that convinced me to go with your dad was his wiener. He had a big one. You inherited that from him."

Liam felt his face go red.

"Sandro, on the other hand, he had a tiny little thing. Could hardly feel it inside me." She raised her voice and yelled toward the kitchen. "Hey, Jeannie? Enzo got a tiny little wiener like his daddy?"

Liam heard Aidan snickering behind him. "I've really gotta go, Ma. You take care of yourself."

"You too, Sonny Boy," she said. "You may be a fairy, but you fight like a real man." She turned to Aidan. "You take care of my boy here."

"You bet I will," Aidan said.

Liam felt all his adrenaline drain away. His right shoulder hurt, and the knuckles of his right fist. It felt like he'd pulled a muscle in his stomach too. Just like he'd said outside, this was why he'd left Jersey. This place, these people—they weren't home to him. His home was wherever Aidan was.

He reached out and took Aidan's hand, and squeezed. "Bye, Ma. I'll Skype you when we get back."

He led the way out the front door to the porch. Frank Barrow was on his porch next door, holding up a six-pack of beer. "You guys want to chill out?" he called.

Liam pulled Aidan along and said, "Get a boyfriend, Frank."

31 – Jersey Boys

"That was the guy you put on the show for?" Aidan asked as they drove away.

"It wasn't a show. I had to strip down anyway, and I guess I felt sorry for the guy."

"You're a prince among men," Aidan said wryly.

"Listen, can you find us a motel near the airport? And then a flight back home?"

"I'm on it. Head for US 1." Aidan already knew where he wanted to go—a luxury hotel across from EWR, where he'd stayed once. He used his phone to make a reservation, then sat back. "I'll look for a flight after we get settled. I hate doing something so complicated on a tiny screen."

"Whatever."

When Liam was in a black mood, he didn't talk. So Aidan looked out the window and remembered all the trips he and his parents had made through this part of the state, en route to family events. The landscape seemed the same at first, the maples and elms lining the roads, the same truck stops and warehouses. But new housing developments had sprung up, abutting glassy office buildings and chain stores. What had been a two-lane road was now a divided highway.

They reached the road Aidan's father had called Useless One, and the part of the state most people thought of when they heard New Jersey—the tangle of highways, oil refineries, and run-down buildings. Aidan knew there was so much more—the verdant, rolling hills around Ellen's home, the '50s motels and acres of sandy beach of Wildwood Crest, the faded Victorians of Cape May, the scrubby Pine Barrens, and the boardwalk at Atlantic City.

New Jersey would always be his home, he thought, no matter where he moved around the globe. He knew the state bird was the American goldfinch, the state flower the blue violet. The Lenni-Lenape Indians had been the original settlers of the Delaware Valley. He had the state's DNA inside him, and that wasn't going to change.

"The airport's up ahead," Liam said, breaking through his reverie. "Where am I going?"

"The Marriott. On the left."

"I don't want anything fancy. Just a place I can crash."

"Here's a news flash, Liam. It's not always all about you."

Liam glared at him. "You can be so gay sometimes, you know that?"

"And you can't be? Having a hissy fit and smacking around your brother-in-law? Who happens to be the son of your mother's ex-boyfriend?"

"Enzo's my ex-brother-in-law," Liam said. "And if you say anything about wieners, I'm putting you out of the car right now."

"Just drive us to the hotel, then."

"I look like some street thug," Liam said. "I can't walk into a hotel lobby like this."

"Sure you can. You take my hand like you did when we walked out of your mother's house, and we stroll right in."

Liam shook his head but navigated the complicated series of traffic lights and turns that took them to the hotel parking lot. He pulled the car into a spot and leaned forward to rest his head on the steering wheel. "I am so tired," he said.

"I know, baby," Aidan said. "We'll check into the room, and you'll have a bath and a nap. And then you'll feel better."

"If you say so."

Liam dragged the two duffels behind him as Aidan strode up to the reservation counter. At times like that he had only to channel Blake Chennault, and he could ignore his and his partner's scruffiness, appear as confident as an Arab sheikh with a billion-dollar bank account. He got the clerk to upgrade him and made sure he got the points for his loyalty account.

Their room was on the eighth floor and faced the airport. Aidan saw the lights of planes taking off and landing, but the double-glazed windows kept the sound out. "I could sleep for a year," Liam said as they walked in.

"Bath first." Aidan turned the water on in the bathroom as Liam flopped onto the bed on his stomach.

"Good position," Aidan said. "Take your shirt off."

Liam complied. Aidan sat beside him on the bed and opened his duffle. He pulled out a bottle of massage oil he'd bought duty-free in Amsterdam and began to rub Liam's shoulders. "Man, that feels good," Liam said, his voice muffled by the pillow.

Aidan jumped up to check the tub. He turned the faucet off and tested the water. Boiling hot. He returned to Liam's side and tugged down his partner's shorts, revealing his luscious ass framed by the white jockstrap. "Don't try anything," Liam mumbled. "I'm too tired."

Aidan massaged his back for a couple of minutes, and Liam drowsed. Then he stood and tried to pull Liam to his feet. He was like dead weight.

"Come on, baby, into the tub," he said. "You need a good soak to relax your muscles."

Liam groaned, but he followed, dropping the jockstrap on the floor. Aidan watched Liam's ass wag as he walked into the bathroom, wanting nothing more than to get down on his knees and stick his tongue up there, but he knew what Liam needed more.

Liam climbed into the tub and sighed contentedly. "This feels so good."

Aidan went out to the bedroom and stripped off his clothes. He plugged his iPhone into the radio and started some New Age music. Then he returned to the bathroom and folded one of the towels, then placed it behind Liam's head. He unwrapped a bar of soap, sat on the bathmat, and lifted Liam's right leg out of the water.

With the soap in his palm, he began with Liam's foot, paying attention to each of the toes, then working his way up to the calf and the thigh, feeling Liam's amazing musculature beneath his hands. Neither of them spoke.

Liam crossed his arms behind his head and rested against the pillow as Aidan repeated the process with Liam's left leg.

Aidan stood and stepped into the tub, then straddled Liam. The music was accompanied by the gentle lapping of the water around Liam's body as Aidan leaned down to soap up his shoulders. Aidan's balls were pulled up and his stiff dick dangled in front of Liam's face, but neither of them made any move toward sex.

He scooted backward and bent down to raise Liam's right arm out of the water. As it dripped, he soaped it up, then lathered his hands and rubbed them under Liam's armpit. "That tickles," Liam said with a slight giggle.

Aidan kissed the top of Liam's head, then moved to the left arm. With his hands full of soap, he massaged Liam's neck, feeling the tight cords there relax under his fingers. Then he pushed Liam's legs aside and sat in the tub.

Liam's dick was as stiff as his own, and they rubbed against each other as Aidan began a careful, sensual massage of his partner's chest. Liam's eyes were closed, his breathing regular. The warm, soapy water eddied around them.

"I want you so bad," Liam said, his eyes still closed. "But I'm so tired."

"What would the SEALs think of you now?" Aidan asked, then leaned forward to kiss him lightly on the lips. "Too tired for sex?"

"I could have a whole platoon lined up naked, and I'd still be too tired," Liam said, his words slow and his voice languid.

Aidan pushed back a few inches and soaped his hands again. Then he reached down into the water to Liam's groin and ran his fingers through the curly hair there, teasing a fingernail down Liam's shaft. Liam moaned softly.

Aidan stroked his partner's perineum; then he rubbed his index finger around Liam's hole for a moment or two.

Then Aidan stood. Water cascaded down his front, back, and sides. "Roll over, Beethoven," he said.

"Too tired," Liam said.

Aidan lifted and tugged Liam's left side, and finally accepting the inevitable, Liam turned onto his stomach. His back was smooth, marred only by a couple of small freckles and a narrow trail of hair that rose from his crack. Aidan squatted over him once more, using the soap to further relax his partner's tense muscles.

The music from the bedroom shifted tempo to something faster and sexier, and Aidan wanted to lie down on top of Liam, feel their bodies so close to each other, then jam his dripping dick into Liam's ass and fuck him until they both exploded in a rapture of semen and soap.

But that would have to wait. He stood once again, feeling his thighs complain, and then helped Liam stand. He looked like a Greek god come to life, Aidan thought as he opened the drain, turned the water back on, and picked up the shower attachment.

Liam stood there at a modified parade rest, his legs apart, his arms dangling at his sides, his dick now half-hard. Aidan tested the water and, when it was warm enough, used the attachment to rinse Liam off. With wicked intent, he moved the gadget close to Liam's groin and drilled his dick and balls with jets of water, then separated the golden cheeks of Liam's ass to spray directly up into his hole.

"You're very sweet," Liam said sleepily.

"I know," Aidan said.

He grabbed a towel and began to dry Liam's body from the top down, first his massive shoulders, his biceps, his pecs. He loved the feel of the gold rings that ran through Liam's nipples.

Like a small child, Liam obediently offered body parts up to a series of towels. Aidan dried his arms, his waist, his dick and balls, then each leg in turn. When he was finished, he led Liam to the king-size bed. He pulled aside the covers, and Liam slid in. Then Aidan tucked him in and kissed his forehead. Liam was asleep before Aidan stood.

He was still naked, and his dick was uncomfortably hard. There was an achiness in his balls he recognized from his younger years when he'd been tantalized by sexy men in movies or at clubs, then gone home without satisfaction. But now he had something to look forward to.

He pulled on one of the complimentary terry-cloth bathrobes and called room service to order dinner, telling them not to bring anything for at least an hour. He turned all the lights off except the standing lamp by the easy chair at the window and settled down there to watch the planes and read until he heard the knock at the door.

He took the tray from the server and carried it over to the round table in the corner of the room. He lifted the lid off a platter of steak and roasted potatoes and breathed in deeply. If he wasn't going to get laid soon, at least he could eat.

The smell of the food woke Liam as Aidan sliced into the steak—medium rare, just the way he liked it.

"How long did I sleep?" Liam asked, sitting up in the bed.

"An hour or so." Aidan got up and handed the other bathrobe to Liam. He grabbed a quick look as Liam stood up naked—he could never get enough of his partner's body.

They sat across from each other at the table and ate. "There's nothing like a good American steak," Liam said.

"And these are Jersey tomatoes," Aidan said, spiking one of the wedges with his fork. "My dad used to get so excited when the first tomatoes ripened in our garden. He'd slice them up and sprinkle them with kosher salt." He leaned forward and offered the wedge to Liam, who opened his mouth and nipped it.

"You can take the boy out of Jersey," he said after tasting the tomato. "But you can't take the Jersey out of the boy."

"Do you think we could stay here a couple of days?" Aidan asked. "Maybe go down the shore? I'd like to drive down to Trenton to the cemetery where my parents are. I know we might not get back here again for a long time."

"If you want, sweetheart," Liam said. He stood, stripped off the robe, and laid it over the back of the chair. Aidan watched his sexy ass as Liam walked back to the bed and then slid under the covers.

Then Aidan put the dishes back on the tray and left it by the door. He expected Liam to fall asleep, but instead his partner sat up. Aidan pulled off his own robe and then slipped in next to Liam, feeling his partner's warmth beside him.

"You know I'd never do anything to hurt you," Liam said.

Aidan shifted on the bed so he was facing his partner. "If I know anything about you, Liam, it's that you are a kind, honest person, and that you have amazing control over your feelings and your actions."

"I really showed that today," Liam said. "Busting Enzo's head."

"Well, okay, sometimes you do lose it," Aidan said. "But that's what I'm here for. To look after you. Just like your mother told me to."

Liam kissed him lightly. "I'm very lucky to have found you."

"Right back at you, sweetheart," Aidan said. He kissed Liam back, harder, then climbed over so that he was sitting on Liam's thighs, his dick hard once again.

Liam's was hard too, and Aidan fisted it. "Where's that oil?" Liam asked.

Aidan leaned over him to reach the oil, and as he did Liam tweaked both Aidan's nipples. Aidan shivered with delight. He tried to return to his position, but Liam wouldn't let him—he kept one arm around Aidan's back and bent forward to nibble at the nubs of brown flesh, first the left, then the right.

Aidan's ass was sitting on top of Liam's dick, and he squirmed around a bit so that the head was poking at his hole. As Liam continued to nibble on his tits, he moved his ass an inch or two forward and back, trying to see if he could get the dick to slip inside him on its own.

Liam groaned, and his fingers kneaded the muscles of Aidan's back. "You're killing me," he said around a mouthful of nipple.

Aidan squirted some massage oil into his palm, then lifted his ass and used one hand to grab Liam's dick, lube it up, and then guide it inside him. There was a moment's discomfort as Liam's beefy dick pushed past his anal ring, but then his body began to float and he relished that full, tight feeling of having his partner inside him.

He looked down at Liam's face. A trickle of sweat dripped down from his forehead, but his eyes were open, focused on Aidan, and the intensity of his gaze rocketed Aidan down to his core. The gentle friction of skin against skin, the heat of Liam's dick raising the temperature of his channel.

Aidan slid down like a fireman on a pole, an analogy that almost always made him giggle. His balls rested on Liam's bush, and the curly hair tickled him. "You think this is funny?" Liam said in mock anger.

Aidan raised his ass an inch or two, then slammed it back down, and Liam yelped. "You want to play rough, do you?"

Liam reached up and twisted Aidan's nipples as Aidan bucked up and down, feeling his partner's dick slide in and out of him. Liam let go of one nipple to reach for Aidan's cock, and as he fisted it in time with Aidan's thrusts, Aidan's world swirled into a kaleidoscope of colors, and everything faded except the amazing feelings rising from his ass and groin.

The windowpane rattled as a plane swooped in low. Aidan whimpered and Liam gasped for breath, and then with a strangled cry Liam shot his load, the hot semen coursing up to tantalize Aidan's prostate, and that was enough to send him over the edge as well.

His thighs were on fire, and though he wanted to stay in that position forever, Liam's dick still in him, he couldn't hold out, and he pulled off and dropped down beside his partner.

Liam curled toward him. "We might have to put off that sightseeing for a day or so," he said.

"Why?"

"Because all I want to do for at least the next twenty-four hours stay here in bed with you."

"That seems like a good plan to me," Aidan said. "Hayam can stay with Madam Serroli. The Fariases can get settled and start their new lives."

"And they all lived happily ever after," Liam mumbled as they snuggled together, closed their eyes, and fell into deep, dreamless sleep.

The next book in the series was one of my favorite ones to write. I was at a conference called Gay Romance Literature (Gay Rom Lit) in Atlanta. While waiting in the buffet line I stood behind a former porn star, there to promote his new line of erotic romance. He wore a loose tank top, and I was fascinated by his shoulder-to-shoulder angel tattoo.

The next morning I went to Starbucks and wrote fifty pages of this book! I hope you find reading *Finding Freddie Venus* as much fun as I had writing it.

Acknowledgments

Many thanks to my friend Elisa Albo and my aunt, Rebecca Fais Globus, for information on Sephardic Jewish history and customs as well as the Ladino language. The book *Ladino Reveries* by Hank Halio, a gift from my aunt, was very helpful.

I appreciate the support of my critique group partners, all of them excellent writers: Miriam Auerbach, PJ Parrish, Sharon Potts, and Christine Jackson. My colleagues at the South Campus of Broward College are also excellent sounding boards for ideas.

As with each of the books in this series, Maryam Salim has provided excellent editorial guidance. Thank-yous also go to all the other editors and proofreaders who've worked on the series, and to the fabulous cover designers who have helped Aidan and Liam come to life.

About the Author

A native of Bucks County, PA, Neil is a graduate of the University of Pennsylvania, Columbia University and Florida International University, where he received his MFA in creative writing. He lives in South Florida with his husband and two rambunctious golden retrievers. He is a four-time finalist for the Lambda Literary Award in Best Gay Mystery and Best Gay Romance.

A professor of English at Broward College's South Campus, he has written and edited many other books; details can be found at his website, **http://www.mahubooks.com**. He is also past president of the Florida chapter of Mystery Writers of America.

Thanks for reading! I'd love to stay in touch with you. Subscribe to one or more of my newsletters at my website, www.mahubooks.com, and I promise I won't spam you!

Follow me at Goodreads to see what I'm reading, and my author page at Facebook where I post news and giveaways.

If you liked this book, please consider posting a brief review at your vendor, at Goodreads and in reader groups. Even a short review help other readers discover books they might like. Thanks!

www.ingramcontent.com/pod-product-compliance
Lightning Source LLC
LaVergne TN
LVHW011948060526
838201LV00061B/4254